T0164797

SLIGHTLY OFF COURSE

ETHEL MCMILIN

IUNIVERSE, INC.
BLOOMINGTON

Slightly off Course

iUniverse books may be ordered through booksellers or by contacting:

iUniverse
1663 Liberty Drive
Bloomington, IN 47403
www.iuniverse.com
1-800-Authors (1-800-288-4677)

ISBN: 978-1-4502-7864-5 (sc)
ISBN: 978-1-4502-7865-2 (ebk)

Library of Congress Control Number: 2010918109

Printed in the United States of America

iUniverse rev. date: 12/2/2010

This book is dedicated to my niece
Kim Guldborg who edits my manuscripts and
Chris Volzer, a pilot, who gave me some good advice.

CHAPTER 1

An Unpleasant Surprise

Bethany did her best to try to be calm, but it wasn't working. She was headed for Europe and was so excited she could hardly sit still. She had entered some contest just for the fun of it and she'd actually won first prize which was a round trip ticket to Europe. Bethany had never won anything in her life and she had a hard time grasping the fact that she really did win and she'd soon be sitting in an airplane on her way to Europe.

In only moments she'd board the airplane. Never had she taken an airplane ride so she was a little nervous along with the excitement. Bethany heard the call for boarding and followed her fellow passengers down the ramp to the airplane. She looked for her seat number—C10. No one was in that row but shortly after she sat down, a young man joined her.

Eric looked at the young woman sitting in the same row where he was assigned to sit. The first thing he did was notice the deep blue eyes and the pretty blonde hair. What a beautiful girl he was going to have as a traveling partner. He smiled at her. "Hello, my name is Eric Johnson. And your name is?" he asked.

"My name is Bethany. This is my first trip and I'm just a little nervous. I've never been on a plane before," she confessed.

"There's nothing to worry about. I've traveled all over the world by air and nothing has ever happened to me. Airplanes are pretty safe these days as they have a lot of inspections to pass. And they have to pass every inspection or the plane doesn't leave the ground," Eric informed her.

"Oh, that's good to know. It looks like everyone is aboard and they're closing the door. Oh, the plane is moving away from the airport." Bethany caught her breath. This was what she was waiting for but why did she have to be so nervous about it.

"The pilot will drive the airplane down the runway until he gets in position for take off but then he'll have to stop and wait for his turn. There are only two planes ahead of us so it will be a short wait. I've been on an airplane when there were ten planes that we had to wait for." Eric hesitated and then he remarked, "If you get frightened, just hang on to me. I won't mind in the least." A young lady as beautiful as Bethany could hang on to him anytime and he sure wouldn't mind a bit.

"I just might do that," Bethany remarked with a grin.

In only a few minutes the plane rolled down the runway at a fast speed and was soon in the air.

"Oh, that leaves a little knot in my stomach," Bethany declared.

"The next time you fly, you won't even notice the movement. You get used to it pretty quickly. Look out the window. We're up above the clouds. When we get to a clear space, you can look down and see how little everything looks. The fields look very neat, more so than when you're on the ground."

"Oh, yes, I can see. You can even see the little cars going down the freeway. They do look small." Bethany stared out the window for some time. This was so interesting. She never thought she'd be up above the clouds but now she was.

Pretty soon she began to get sleepy and decided to take a nap. It looked like Eric was about half asleep already. It was an early flight and they had to be at the airport an hour earlier than the flight time. She wasn't exactly used to getting up at four o'clock in the morning.

Since the plane wasn't full, Eric found several pillows and blankets and gave them to her so she could fit them around her just right and be comfortable. She said thanks to him and made herself comfortable.

She lean back hoping she could go to sleep so she wouldn't have jet lag when she arrived in Europe. In just minutes, the girl was in a deep sleep oblivious to anything around her.

Meanwhile, the pilots were having a rough time. A small plane rammed into their plane and knocked out the intercom to the passengers and damaged the plane considerably. There was no way to warn the passengers. Both the pilot and the copilot were dazed by the accident but the pilot managed to steer the plane in a direction hoping to find an island. He wasn't sure they would reach the island before the plane went down. The copilot passed out from the hit he had taken and didn't awaken. The pilot was barely conscious but he did his best to stay awake. His head hurt something awful but he didn't have time to take any medication.

While Bethany was sleeping, somewhere in the back of her mind she heard loud noises and felt herself jerked around somewhat. She was so deep in sleep that the noise didn't wake her up. It was part of her dream, she thought. Suddenly her feet were getting cold. Water was coming into the airplane. Why were her feet in cold water? She woke up with a start. She stood up and looked down on the floor. Water really was seeping into the airplane!

Where was Eric? Bethany noticed that people were headed for the door hoping to make it out before the water filled the plane and she decided that would be the right thing to do. But the plane didn't seem to be sinking anymore.

She noticed that some people were jumping out the door into the water. One guess she had was that water would be very cold. Bethany was glad she could swim but how far did she have to swim in order to reach land. When she reached the door, she realized that the plane had landed in water very near the shore. She sighed a sigh of relief. That was good. She sure didn't like the idea of swimming with all of her clothes on for a long distance.

Before she jumped, Bethany looked to see if she could help anyone else. Most of the people seemed to be sleeping. Or were they…?

Eric, where was Eric? He wasn't in his seat. When did he get off? Why didn't he wake her? She thought he was going to take care of her. Some of the people didn't appear to be breathing. Should she help them? She touched the passenger closest to the door. She shook him and he fell over. Bethany screamed. No one woke up or started to get up even after her scream. Were all those people dead? If they were, how did she happen to escape death? Was she having a nightmare?

As she looked more closely, she noticed cuts and blood covering most of the people whose faces she could see. Some of the luggage in the overhead compartments had fallen on the passengers. Some people were tossed around and landed on others because they didn't have their seat belts on or they must have been in the aisle when the plane crashed, she assumed. She heard someone coming up behind her.

"I've checked all the people still on the plane, Bethany. They're dead. The ones who survived have already jumped off the plane. I think that perhaps we should do that as well," Eric stated as he patted her shoulder.

"I'm so glad you're here. Do you have any idea what happened?" she asked almost not wanting to know. Her first airplane ride and it ended in a crash! So much for airplanes being safe now days as Eric had said before they left the airport.

"A smaller plane flew right into ours, Bethany. It was while we were in the clouds and if I were to guess, I'd say that the small airplane lost its directional equipment. It went down in the middle of the ocean and I'm pretty sure none of the passengers survived. Our pilot headed in this direction hoping to find an island and run it up on the shore. We managed to land in water not too deep. I think the pilot wanted to land on the beach and run over the trees but he crashed into the huge trees instead. They were too big for the airplane. I'm just guessing. I knew when the small plane hit the front of our airplane. I was looking out the window. When we crashed I was in the bathroom."

"Why did those other passengers die?" Bethany asked.

"The question should be why did we survive? It was a hard impact and most of the passengers hit their head so hard that it did them in. Some were walking to the bathroom and waiting to get in and they were thrown all over and landed on other people. Some of the luggage landed on people as well. The plane buckled a little upon impact and that opened some of the luggage compartments. Then some people didn't bother to keep their seat belts fastened and of course the crash threw them all over. The crash was so hard that it's a wonder the plane didn't buckle into two pieces."

"Let's get out of this airplane if you're sure that we can't do anything for the rest of the people," Bethany suggested. "They're sure bloodied and banged up. It's an awful sight to see. The only thing I can think that saved me is that I had several pillows around me and was fastened in tight. But I'm sure some of those other people must have been too. Or maybe I was just sitting in a better place when the impact took place."

When she reached the door, she stopped just before she jumped. It was a ways down there, but there was no other way out. The water couldn't be too deep since the plane didn't fill up with water. Finally she worked up the nerve to jump and hoped all would be well when she hit the water. It was so cold that it definitely chilled her, but she jumped out prepared to swim for the shore but then she realized that she could walk out of the water. It was only about waist deep. She was a little dazed from what happened.

Eric was right behind her making sure that she was okay when she jumped. It was nice to have someone who knew what they were doing to guide her. Somehow it made her feel a little better. She was a grown woman and could take care of herself but she'd never been in a situation like this. She wouldn't be opposed to some help or suggestions.

"Just be glad that it's nice and sunny out today so that our clothes will dry quickly," her new friend told her and smiled. He knew that she was nervous and upset and so was everyone else that had survived. Eric had counted about seven people who jumped out of the plane including Bethany and him. There were only thirty people on board including the flight attendants and the pilots. The plane was far from full.

When Eric was out of the water and on the shore he looked at the group of people who looked almost stunned. They needed a little leadership and encouragement right now before someone panicked.

Before he could say anything, one of the survivors remarked rather sarcastically, "I don't think we're in Kansas, Toto." The man looked at Eric and just shook his head. "I'm Dennis."

Eric smiled. There was always a comic in the group and that wouldn't hurt anything in the present situation. Even in their nervous condition, everyone had smiled or laughed at his comment. "I'm Eric Johnson. I think the first thing we should do is all sit down and talk about what happened. We need to make some plans. Is there any one of you that knows how to operate the radio on the airplane so that we may call for help? That's if the radio is still working."

No hands went up.

"Just who made you in charge?" a man with a frown on his face asked while he glared at Eric.

"I'm sorry but I'm not in charge. I'm trying to arrange a meeting where we can all talk and decide what we should to do. Your name is Albert at least that's what is written on your tee shirt." Albert was a tall man with a healthy head of dark brown hair—certainly the tallest one of the group. He looked as though he could be a little intimidating, but Eric wasn't about to be intimidated by the man.

"Yeah, I'm Albert, Albert Desmond. And I think we should vote on who is going to be in charge."

"Well, Albert Desmond, it's a little hard to vote on people we don't know anything about. Right now we don't even know each other's names. Suppose you tell me a little about yourself and what your expertise is."

"You mean what I'm good at? I'm good at bossing people around," he stated in a smart aleck manner.

It took all Eric had to be decent to the young man. Now was the time to be cooperative and not try to be funny. "Well, we shall call on you if we need any bossing around. Now suppose the rest of you tell the group who you are and what you're good at that might help us in this situation. Does anyone know anything about what's good to eat and what isn't when it comes to plants?"

A rather tall young woman with long brown hair and with some freckles on her attractive face spoke up. "I know all about searching the woods for food, Eric. I've had wilderness training and I was raised looking for good things to eat in the wilderness. My name is Leslie Morris. This place looks very green and it would be my guess that there are lots of edible plants around this area."

"Terrific. I knew you were a smart gal as soon as I laid my eyes on you. Now who wants to be next?"

"I'm Jim Majors," said a slim man with reddish blonde hair. "I know a little about electronics but I don't know anything about airplane radios. But I'd give it a try if there isn't anyone else who knows anything about electronics."

"That's good to hear. I know a little also and perhaps between the two of us we may just figure out how to use it. Now who wants to be next?"

"I'm Bethany McMillan. I'm a good cook but I'd need something to cook. Do you really think we'll be here long enough to worry about gathering food from the fields? Don't you think there is enough food on the airplane?"

"Bethany, we don't know. If they have tracked us, we should have help today. But if something happened to whatever they use to track airplanes they wouldn't be able to find us. No telling what happened to any equipment when we hit the water and those trees. No one knows at this point. We don't know if the pilot called in a May Day or not," Eric remarked and hesitated as he looked at the worried group.

"So I think the best thing for us to do is to plan on a future here for sometime and then hope they show up today or tomorrow. I'm certain they'll come looking for us but they may not know where to look. It certainly isn't going to do us any harm to look around for edible food just in case. If we don't need it, we'll at least have had some good exercise going into the field and gathering it." Before he finished talking Albert interrupted him.

"Me, I want to go back into the plane and get the food that's in there and have a feast on it. That's what we should do! We paid our money for this airplane ride so therefore we have a right to that food." Albert declared.

"You mean eat it all today and then what will we have to eat tomorrow?" Bethany asked the man.

"We'll be rescued by then. You all know we'll be so why not have a party now with all of the food on the plane?" he replied.

"Albert, we don't know when or if we'll be rescued. It never hurts to plan on having something for tomorrow. Now, we have to make some type of ladder to get back into the airplane. Would you help with the ladder, Albert? We can get those poles that are lying around amongst the trees and put together a make-shift ladder by tying them together with vines," Eric declared.

"I'm not working on some useless project. Get someone else," Albert remarked defiantly and folded his arms and glared at Eric. He said he wasn't in charge but he was sure acting like he was.

"I know all about making make-shift ladders. We did that in boy scouts. I'm Dennis Williams," exclaimed the man with brunette hair and pleasant looking facial features. "Perhaps Peter Jameson here can help me. We're good friends. If it's alright with you Eric, we'll start on that right now."

Eric looked over at the man with black hair who hadn't said much. Peter nodded his head in agreement.

"That's great. Now let's…"

"By the way, I vote for you to be the leader of the group," interrupted Dennis. "All who agree that we need a leader and that Eric is the one please raise your hand." Dennis made the suggestion as he knew they were a lot better off with some one in charge and Eric seemed to be someone who was capable of leading a group of stranded people. He liked the suggestions the man had made.

Five hands went up. Albert glared at everyone. He should be the leader. He was better at it than anyone there. If he were the leader they'd just sit down and wait until someone came after them which would be tonight or early tomorrow. All of this silly planning didn't make a bit of sense to him. But he said nothing more. He'd looked at some of the people's faces when he suggested a party. He guessed that was the wrong thing to say. No one thought this was a time to have a party and especially not with so many people on the airplane that didn't survive.

"All right, I accept but remember we're all in this together. Let's all decide just what we need to do in case we're here for a few days. I hope Albert is right and our rescuers will be here tonight or in the morning. That would be the best thing, but I know that sometimes they have a hard time locating planes that go down. I'm a little concerned because the plane hit those trees so hard that I don't know if the tracking equipment survived long enough to let our airport officials know where we are."

Jim spoke up. "We could try to find it and see. But it won't be easy as we don't have any tools to work with. Perhaps in time we'll find something on the island that we can use to help open up the airplane and look at the engine and find the instrument that is used to track airplanes. I sure don't know what to look for. If it was working we sure wouldn't have any problems."

Albert looked at them and shook his head. They sure were making plans to stay on the island for some time. Well he had no such plans. They would be rescued by tonight or early tomorrow morning at the latest. He'd just sit and let them make their plans and watch them do a bunch of useless tasks. There was no way he was going to enter into this foolishness.

Bethany looked at Eric. He seemed to have a lot of confidence in what he was doing. That made her relax just a little more. At least she felt as though she knew Eric even though she didn't know anyone else. She was glad to see another female in the group. She would be getting acquainted with Leslie shortly as the two would likely be the ones who gathered the food and cooked it. It was terrible what had just happened, but she was pleased to be one of the survivors.

Dennis had been impressed with Eric. Even when he wasn't the leader, he'd given them a lot of ideas about what to do. He was impressed how he'd helped Bethany through the whole situation. That girl had to be frightened. There wasn't any doubt but that Eric would be a good leader.

On the other hand, he'd never met anyone quite like Albert. That man had a chip on his shoulder and was just waiting for someone to knock it off. Well, it wouldn't be him. He'd stay away from the man as much as possible. There was plenty of room on the island so he wouldn't have to get too close to the disagreeable individual.

Dennis watched the others as they talked and worked. With the exception of Albert, it seemed that they had a pretty good group of people. That was good if they were forced into an extended stay on the island.

CHAPTER 2

Building a Shelter

When everyone was seated, Eric began to talk about some of the ideas he thought they should think about in case they were stranded on the island more than a day or two. He would ask everyone's opinion and have a full discussion a little later.

"Now who wants to fix a shelter for us in case it should rain or we have a storm or something where we need to get to a safe and dry place?" Eric asked.

"I'll help make a shelter, Eric," Bethany offered.

"You can count me in," Leslie promised.

"We need more than two ladies if we are going to make a good shelter. Dennis and Peter are working on the ladder. When they get through they can help with the shelter. Jim and I are going to work on getting the radio fixed so we can send a signal. We have to find something that will work as tools. Leslie you can help Bethany with a shelter but you need a man for some of the heavy work. The only one left is Albert." Eric looked at the man and Albert quickly looked away.

Bethany walked over to Albert and smiled at him. "Let's make this a game, Albert, even though we know that we'll possibly be rescued today or tomorrow. But let's just do it for fun," she exclaimed and took hold of his hand and lifted him off the stump he was sitting on. "You can be the boss as I have a feeling that you have built buildings in the past and you would know how to get started. Leslie and I don't have the faintest idea how to start a shelter but we sure would do whatever you ask us if we can."

Albert couldn't resist the pretty young lady and he reluctantly stood up and walked with her to find a good place for a shelter. He loved the touch of her hand. No one else in the rescue group could persuade him to help but he just melted when Bethany asked him to supervise the work.

Eric smiled. Bethany evidentially had a little psychology and knew how to handle a man like Albert. But then, if the beautiful girl asked him to do something, he would probably do it also. She was a very pretty girl with a winning way and a very winning smile. He couldn't imagine anyone turning Bethany down when she asked them for a favor.

Jim and Eric started talking about the radio and what they each knew about electronics. They looked around for a sharp rock in case they needed to cut something. If they had to clamp something together, they'd need two rocks. They also gathered some vines to use as string. It all may be unnecessary but just in case they needed to tie something together, they would have the vines for that.

Eric checked on the ladder. It was coming along and soon would be finished, Peter informed him. Probably in less than an hour the ladder would be ready to use. It wasn't the best looking ladder he had ever seen but it would work.

Then Eric thought about something else. All those people on the airplane that had died in the crash, what would they do with them if they weren't rescued in a day or two? The smell would be unbearable. Something would have to be done tomorrow at the latest for sure.

"Jim, have you thought about what to do with the bodies of the people who didn't survive and are still on the airplane?"

"Yes, and if we don't hear anything by tomorrow, we need to bury them. We'll be rescued today or tomorrow if they tracked us. If not the stench from those who didn't survive would be so terrible we won't be able to stand to go into the airplane. There are things on that plane that we need for our shelter and survival. We should think about what to do. We could dig one big grave and bury them all in one so that when we're rescued we can show the airline officials where they are. What do you think?"

"Good idea, Jim. If we can't get through to anyone and if we hear nothing from them, then tomorrow we'll start digging. But what will we dig with. Perhaps we can find a large hole of some type and put branches and as much dirt as we can dig with our hands to cover the bodies. We can't hurt them any more. It's a shame that so many died but the way the plane crashed, I can't believe that the seven of us survived unhurt at that except for a few bruises. Someone was watching out for us," Eric stated.

"Yes, it's like God protected us because it wasn't our time as yet," Jim remarked soberly.

"I believe you're right," Eric agreed. "I agree completely. For some reason God chose us seven to live. Perhaps some day we'll find out why we survived the crash when so many others died."

"One thing we have to do, friends, is to find a stream. The bottled water on the airplane will only last a few days. Does anyone know how to locate water?" Eric asked.

"I know how to do that, "Leslie spoke up. "Bethany and I shall take a walk and find a spring as soon as Peter and Dennis are free to help with the shelter. But what are we going to carry the water in? We need to find some container on the plane that we can bring the water back to our shelter."

"You find the spring and we'll find a way to get it back here," Eric promised. It was good to have Leslie in their group. She was one talented girl when it came to living in the wilderness and that was what they'd be doing if they weren't rescued today or tomorrow.

It wasn't too long before the ladder was built. After that project was finished, Peter and Dennis carried it out into the water and leaned it against the opening door of the airplane.

"I wouldn't let more than one person at a time step on the ladder. We don't know how well the vines will hold up," Dennis warned the two men. Then Peter and Dennis immediately started working on the shelter.

They told the ladies to go look for water. They had made a lot of progress in constructing the building. While Albert did help, he mostly told them how and what to do. The two men decided that the man knew what he was talking about and took orders from him without questions. They wondered if Albert was a carpenter or something along that line.

The two young women started walking up the hill a ways. Leslie stopped after they had only gone a short distance. "See the way the land is there, Bethany? There is water in that spot. Let's go check it out. It's good that it's so close to our camp. We may need to come back with some type of equipment and dig a little, but there is water right there. All the signs are pointing right to it."

Bethany wondered how she knew that but then she had told her that she often camped out. Well, she should know what she was talking about then. To Bethany it just looked like any other piece of land around the area.

Leslie walked to the spot. She found a sharp stick and stuck it in the ground. Immediately, there was water spewing out.

"Let's go back and tell the men that we found water to drink!" Leslie stated. She knew there had to be plenty of water around somewhere since there was green grass all over the area. She wasn't the least bit worried about finding some. There was no reason for it not to be good drinking water since there was nobody on the island to pollute it. Finding the water so close to the shelter pleased her. Water was one item that they'd need a lot of for cooking, drinking and bathing.

"That sure didn't take you long," Bethany remarked. "I'm impressed. You didn't just learn that when you were camping, did you?"

"No, I took a course in wilderness survival. It was really interesting and one of the first things they showed us was how to find water. I was told that in the Bible people like Jacob and his descendants doused for water."

"Yes, I remember reading that. They took sticks from certain trees and held them over spots and if there was water there, the sticks would move. My dad even tried it once over a well on our friends' place and it worked. It was fascinating. I guess God wanted people to be able to find water so He made a way."

"I've heard that there are different currents in the earth—one for water another for oil and for iron and other things. If we just knew the right equipment to find the currents, we could find a lot of things," Leslie exclaimed.

"That's an interesting thing to know," Bethany replied. She had an idea that she could learn a lot from Leslie about surviving in the wilderness. She wasn't too anxious to be here for a long time, but she was pleased that God had put Leslie in the group of survivors. They were going to at least have something to eat and water to drink with her around.

The ladies slowly walked back down the hill to the camp. They talked as they did and were getting a little better acquainted with each other. Leslie realized that Bethany was a Christian so she'd be careful what she said. She had never paid a lot of attention to church or God but she would respect Bethany's beliefs. She liked her right from the start.

CHAPTER 3

The Makeshift Shelter

Bethany and Leslie returned with the good news that water was only a few yards away and it would be no problem getting nice cool spring water to drink. Eric was pleased and promised to find something in the airplane that would allow them to carry water to the shelter.

"I'll give the ladder a try first," Jim offered and started climbing up the steps very carefully. It seemed to be pretty sturdy so far. He reached the door to the plane and stepped in. Jim was a little relieved. He wasn't too sure that the vines would hold his weight and was pleased that it did. He tried to get into where the pilot and copilot were but the door was barred. It wasn't going to be easy to open.

"Eric, the door is jammed. The lock is broken. I can't get into the cockpit. Do you have any suggestions?"

Before he could answer, Leslie spoke up. "I used to be a flight attendant. Let me see if I can help," she announced.

"Come on up," Jim suggested.

"Eric, are you ready to come up after Leslie does?"

"I'm ready," he answered.

Leslie made her way up the ladder and saw the jammed door to the cockpit. She suggested that they find the weak spot and stick a board in there and force it. Leslie watched and helped the two men force the jammed door open. When it opened, what she saw in the cockpit made her scream and back out and away. She began to sob uncontrollably. Oh, she didn't want to see that scene again. It was bad enough to see the people in the airplane that were dead, but those poor pilots.

Jim put his arm around the girl. "Thanks, Leslie. Thanks for helping us force open that door. I'm sorry you had to see that horrible scene with the pilot and copilot. But you did a good job. Now do you want to sit down a minute?"

"No, I want to get out of here and go back to land. Those poor men were crushed. Oh, what an awful sight that is," Leslie managed to say and trembled as she hurried down the ladder. She had to do something to get that scene out of her mind. The heads of the pilots were smashed right into the plane's instruments. She wished she'd never volunteered to help.

Why hadn't she just made her suggestion and left the plane. Leslie felt that everything in her stomach was about to come up. She'd seen a lot of things in her travels but nothing like that scene in the pilot's cockpit. Oh, those poor men didn't have a chance to survive.

She hurried over to where Albert, Bethany, and the others were working and started to help. Perhaps if she got involved in making the shelter again, she could forget the terrible scene she had just seen. The only thing she could think of that was good was they must have died instantly as bad as cockpit looked. They wouldn't have suffered she was quite sure. She wiped the tears out of her eyes and worked hard at helping with the shelter.

"Leslie is pretty shook up from looking in the cockpit at the pilot and copilot. I hope she can forget the sight. I thought she was going to pass out for a moment when she first saw the pilots. Just take another look. Getting to the radio isn't going to be as easy as we thought. I think we have to take those two men out of there first."

Eric looked at the sight and groaned. It wouldn't be an easy thing to do. He tried to think what the best way to get to the radio would be. The only way was to remove the pilot and copilot's crushed bodies.

"Shall we lift the pilot and copilot and put them in with the rest of the people?" Jim asked.

"Let's find a blanket and wrap each of them. Otherwise, we are going to be all bloody and we have no other clothes at this point."

"You're right, Eric." They found the blanket and wrapped the pilot in it and placed him in an empty seat and then did the same for the copilot. It wasn't pleasant. Eric gagged some but managed to finish the job. Jim took it in his stride. Eric was surprised that it didn't bother Jim as much as it did him.

Finding some bottles of water and a wash rag, Eric wiped the blood off the instruments. The panel looked so foreign to him. He had used car radios some time back. There ought to be a few things similar between car and airplane radios.

"Eric, do you have a cell phone?" Jim asked.

"Yes, let me try to see if I can get a signal." He walked over to the door and started to call but a no signal sign came on. "I guess cell phones are out unless someone has a better one than I have. Or perhaps if someone were to climb a tree... You can never tell but it was worth a try."

"Jim, can you make heads or tales out of those instruments?"

"Yes, this is the radio right here. I wonder if there would be some type of manual in one of these compartments to tell us how this works. You look and I'll push a few buttons. To tell the truth, it looks like the radio has been damaged, but it might be possible that we can fix it." Jim pushed a few buttons and nothing happened. He held down the speaker that would allow him to contact somebody in case the radio was in working condition.

"May day, May day," he kept repeating and then lifted his hand. Absolutely no reply! He tried several other things but nothing worked. He began to take a few things apart to look at what was inside. He shook his head.

"Hey, Jim, I found the manual. Let's see if we can get that radio working by reading the manual. It ought to have some good information in it."

Jim said nothing. He already knew it wasn't going to work unless they could find some parts for it, but he let Eric give it a try just in case he was wrong.

Eric followed the manual exactly, but nothing happened. He repeated it again and again and then shook his head. "I wonder why it isn't working."

"Eric, it has been crushed. I suggest that we take it out of the plane and work on it down there and see if we can repair the parts. I have no idea if we can or not but if we could just send some type of signal, the people in the airport tower would know where we were," Jim suggested. "Or someone would receive our signal and perhaps inform the tower."

"You go ahead and do that. I'm going to look and see what food we have here. I don't know about you but I'm hungry." Eric walked over to the galley where he knew the food was kept. There wasn't a lot but there were snacks and some drinks. He decided to leave the liquor in the plane. One thing they didn't need was a bunch of drunks. He was against liquor to start with and had no intentions of telling anyone about how much was there. It could always be used for medicinal purposes in case someone received cuts that could become infected. He pushed the liquor back and behind the cupboard so it couldn't be easily found. Eric took almost all of the edibles he could find. He thought it best to leave some food hidden just in case some of the survivors had heavy appetites.

There were some garbage sacks that the flight attendants always brought around to everyone to dispose of their empty cartons. He put the food in them. When he finished he had about 10 small bags of food. That would be a good start. He wouldn't take them all down for now. The plane was definitely cooler than outside and the food would be better left here for a while.

"How are you doing, Jim?" Eric asked.

"It's going to take a while. I want to look at some of the extra things that are here in the plane that might help us fix this radio. I'll be a while. Why don't you go down and feed that hungry mob before someone faints for lack of food? Or, if you don't feed them you might have a riot on your hands."

"I'll do that, Jim, and then I'll come back up. It's getting a little late and I hope Albert and the girls have made some type of refuge for us. Perhaps I should take the blankets and pillows down first."

Eric gathered some more trash bags and put the blankets in them. He took all he could find. Then he took the pillows. Finally, he took the seat cushions off some of the empty seats. These could be used to make some beds.

"Leslie, please come here a minute," he called.

"What do you need, Eric?" she answered.

"I want you to catch these trash bags. They are full of blanket and pillows. It looks as though we're going to spend the night as it's getting late." Eric tossed them out one at a time and Dennis and Peter came to help. Then he decided to send the food down as well. The idea of it being in with the people who died left an uneasy feeling. So the trash bags were carried over to the shelter that the five people had been working on. Only a small amount was left in the cabinet and out of sight.

Eric went down the ladder and walked over to the shelter. He was impressed. "You all have done a terrific job. I didn't know you could make such a good shelter out of just the fallen trees."

"Well, Albert here is a carpenter among many other things. We let him be the boss and we did the work although he really did help. He's quite good at bossing just like he told us. We found sharp rocks that would cut what we needed and stuffed some dirt around the poles that Albert said would help hold the poles together and not let the rain in. We are pretty proud of our selves," Dennis remarked. Then he added, "We even made a little house out back."

"A little house out back, whatever for?" Eric asked and immediately was embarrassed. They had to have some type of toilet. "Very good, that's something that we'll definitely need. You've done a great job. With this group of people, we shall survive this crash and be a little more comfortable at that."

"The seat in the little house out back is a little rough. If you can find something on the plane to soften it, that would help. Some type of plastic would do fine," Dennis suggested.

"I'll bring some down the next trip. You should all be proud of yourselves. This is a great refuge. Thanks, Albert, for all your advice. Now does anyone have a cell phone?" Eric asked.

All hands went up. "But we all tried to call and the phones just came up with no signal," Leslie informed him.

"I wonder if there'd be any signal at the top or a ways up in that tall tree," Eric asked. "At least the signal wouldn't be interrupted. But who knows how to climb up a tree safely?"

"It won't do any good," Albert remarked. "I have a very expensive cell phone with all the works on it, but it still comes up with no signal. I don't see how it would help to climb higher."

"I heard that it would," Leslie remarked. "Would you tell me how to use your phone and let me climb the tree at least part of the way up and see if it would work, Albert?" she asked carefully. She knew you had to handle with kid gloves.

"Just don't drop it," he ordered rather sternly. He didn't like other people using his cell phone but in this case, he supposed he should cooperate.

Leslie took the phone and put it around her neck. It was good it had a strap on it. She'd never be able to climb if she had to carry it in her hand. She headed up about three-fourths of the tree's height. She dialed 911 on Albert's phone. Although she could hear someone talking, it appeared to be a different language than English. It almost sounded like Spanish or French, neither of which she could understand or converse enough to make sense. On top of that she could barely hear what the man on the other end of the line was saying.

"Is there anyone down there that can speak a foreign language?" she asked.

"I know a little Spanish," Albert conceded. "However, I don't like heights and no way are you going to get me up there. No way!"

"Anyone else?" Leslie asked.

No one responded.

"Come on down for now. If we get real desperate later on, perhaps we can climb a mountain and Albert can try then. Just be careful Leslie, although I'm a medic I sure can't do much for a broken neck or back," Eric admitted.

"Well, it's nice to know we have a medic in our midst" Dennis quipped. "Say Doc, what can you do anything for my..." Dennis started to say.

"Absolutely nothing as there is nothing wrong with you," Eric exclaimed and then laughed with Dennis. It wasn't hard to see who was going to be the joker in the bunch. He had a comment for almost everything.

Leslie carefully climbed back down. It was good to know that they did reach some place even if the number wasn't in the United States.

"We'll wait and see if we get picked up tomorrow before we call on the French or the Spanish people or maybe they were Italians. Right now we should all gather around and eat some food. I'm starved and I have a feeling the rest of you are too."

Eric placed the food on the makeshift table that the five workers had constructed while he and Jim were in the airplane. He put out seven different plates of food. There were some nutrition bars, some cookies, and some pretzels. He also put one can of orange juice by each place.

"Now, if you don't mind, I'd like to thank God for this food. We could have been stuck here without anything but instead we have something to eat." Eric bowed his head and prayed. He knew that Jim did as well but he didn't know about the rest.

"Of all the silly things to do," Albert griped when Eric finished the prayer. "You're an intelligent man and you think that God can hear you or is even interesting in any of us. If there is a God, He certainly wouldn't be watching us. I hope we don't have to put up with a lot of that nonsense while we're stuck here."

"Some of us are used to praying over our food, Albert. It doesn't hurt and you don't have to listen. Just be patient with us, okay?" Bethany remarked sweetly and smiled at Albert.

Albert returned the smile and said no more. He didn't want to make Bethany upset with him. Right now she was the only one that had much to do with him outside of working together on the shelter. She sure was the most beautiful girl he had ever seen. He had every intentions of getting better acquainted with her. Not only that, it seemed impossible to say no to her. Her smile just melted any antagonism that he might have against the rest of the group.

Eric was pleased. At least three of the peopled who survived were Christians. He wondered if there were any more. Leslie had never said anything and she looked rather strange after he prayed. Dennis and Peter never made any remarks either. He was curious where they stood. At least they didn't oppose his pray in the manner that Mr. Albert Desmond did.

After they had eaten, they began to take the airplane seat cushions out of the sacks that Eric had thrown down and make them into beds. Albert helped since he realized that no one was going to rescue them by the time they needed a bed. It was too dark for anyone to try to find them tonight. He was a little disappointed as he was positive they would be rescued in a short time. Well, there was always tomorrow.

Eric was pleased that the group didn't complain about the short rations he had given them. He just had this feeling that the rescue group wasn't going to be coming in the next day or two. If they did, that would be great, but in the back of his mind, he didn't believe they'd be able to find them so quickly without the tracking equipment working properly. Was there a tracking system? He wasn't sure.

"You seemed to be in deep thought, my friend," Jim remarked.

"I just have this feeling that we're going to be here longer than just tomorrow. I don't see how they're going to find us without some type of signal. I think our pilots flew us slightly off course after hitting the small plane. They wouldn't likely be looking for us right here."

"I think you're right," Jim agreed. "We do need to prepare ourselves. We could easily be here for two or three weeks."

CHAPTER 4

The Burial Place

The seat cushions did make into fairly comfortable beds even though the beds were very slim. Everyone had a pillow and a few blankets from the plane and seemed to be comfortable enough to drop off to sleep.

When it was real quiet and apparently all the survivors were sound asleep, they woke up to a horrifying scream. Eric realized that the sound was coming from Leslie. He pushed back the blanket that divided the men from the women. He went over to her bed and gently woke her up. Leslie broke down and sobbed. Eric was sure that she had a nightmare from the scene she had witnessed in the cockpit of the plane that day.

"I'm sorry," she cried, "but I was watching the pilot and copilot get all broken up and I was in the middle of it all. I wonder if I will ever forget that terrible scene with those poor men's heads mashed right into the instruments in the cockpit. Oh..."

Albert spoke up. "Leslie, go to sleep thinking about something nice. For instance, think about when you get back home and see your parents. You told me they were very good people. Now go back to sleep thinking of them and all the fun you've had with them through the years."

"I'll try," Leslie promised and lay back down wondering how she could rid that horrible scene from her memory.

Eric was amazed. He didn't think Albert had a decent feeling in him, but the advice he gave to Leslie was good. If she dwelt on good times most likely that would be what she'd dream about. He had an idea that as she lay in the bed she was thinking about the scene in the cockpit. She needed to dwell on something else.

It wasn't too long before everyone was back to sleep. They'd found some flashlights in the plane but knew they shouldn't use them unless it was absolutely necessary. There may come a time when they really needed a light for something specific and they would save the batteries until then.

In the morning, Eric passed out the food again. Once again he prayed over it. This time Albert only frowned but said nothing. No one complained that they didn't have enough or that they didn't like the rations. They knew it would do them no good. From what Eric could figure, he had about five or six days worth of food before they ran out of the airplane supplies. It was only snack type food, but it was food.

He was a little concerned about water but then he remembered that Leslie had found a spring and he needed to find a container to bring the water into the shelter. It sure didn't take but a few minutes when Leslie was on the scouting trip to find water. He did have some bottles of water that were in the airplane but that wouldn't last very long. They should save the bottles and go to the spring and refill them. He suggested that to his fellow survivors and they agreed.

"Well, what's on the agenda today," Bethany asked.

"We're going to bury the people that are in the airplane. I know it will be gruesome but we may need what's in the airplane for survival and in another day we won't be able to stand going in there. I took a short walk and found a hole. We'll put them in there. It will only be a temporary grave because when they find us, someone will come and dig them up and take them home so their relatives can give them a decent burial. But in the meantime, we'll make just one big grave."

He didn't want Bethany or Leslie involved with the corpses. "I suggest that Leslie and Bethany go and look for food in the woods. But don't get lost," Eric demanded. The last thing he needed at this point was to have to scout the woods for two lost young women. "Take one of the garbage bags or whatever else you can find and use that to bring us some food."

"Don't worry, Eric, I don't get turned around. I've traversed a good many forests in my survival training. We won't get lost," Leslie promised. The girls left immediately as they weren't anxious to view just how the men were going to get the bodies out of the airplane and into a hole. Looking for food was a much better thing to do, they both decided. They'd take their time and hope that the men would be through with their task by the time they returned with the food.

Dennis, Jim, Peter and Eric headed for the airplane. Albert didn't move.

"How are you going to do this," Albert grumbled. "You think that you're going to carry each person down a make shift ladder? It will never hold yours and their weights combined."

"No, I think that we'll let them fall into the water and someone can help float them down the shoreline until they come to the hole I was talking about. Then we'll place them in there. We'll float them all down there first," Eric informed everyone who was listening carefully but not exactly enthusiastic about their task.

Albert had to admit that that was a pretty good solution to the problem. He was impressed with what Eric said. Perhaps he was a good leader after all.

Jim and Dennis climbed into the plane and one by one, they dropped the people in the water until all twenty three of them were out of the plane. Then the men guided the bodies down to where the large hole was located. The bodies had already begun to have a smell but not as bad as it would be in another day. This was a job that couldn't be put off another day.

Eric was pleased when he saw Albert help the bodies float down close to the shore. Finally all the ones that didn't survive had reached the specified place. Now the hard task of picking them up and placing them in the hole would begin. The hole was about six feet wide and several feet deep. Sometimes it took four men to list the heavier corpses.

After the bodies were all in the huge grave, they covered them with poles, leaves, dirt and everything they could find to hide them from animals and prevent the smell from coming up and into their camp. It was all they could do for the people who didn't survive the crash.

Eric told everyone that they should wash up really good. "Use some of the sand as soap and try to wash your hands and arms thoroughly," he suggested.

After everyone washed up Peter and Albert headed for the shelter to see what the next duty would be. By this time Albert was beginning to think that it was going to take longer to get rescued than he thought so he decided he better cooperate with the others. He realized the airplane had things in it they needed and the bodies had to be buried if they were going to go in and out of the airplane. He had a very sensitive nose and it was all he could do to help direct the bodies down the water's edge.

Jim and Eric stayed for a few minutes and said a pray over the grave. When Dennis saw what was going on, he came back and joined them.

"I just thought that we should say a prayer. I want to quote a scripture," Eric stated and he quoted John 3:16 and then said the Lord's Prayer. Then he prayed for the relatives of the ones who didn't survive.

"I'm sure glad that if I had to be stuck out here on this island that I was stuck with some Christian men," Dennis remarked. He shook hands with the two and they all headed back to the shelter.

"What do you think we should do next?" Dennis asked.

"I think we should go up into the plane and open the door and the emergency doors and see if we can get the airplane to smell a little better. We should take some of that cleaning fluid that they clean the airplane with and clean every seat. That will make the air in there smell much better. It will also get rid of any potential disease from the bodies," Eric answered.

"That's a good idea," Dennis exclaimed. "There's a little smell in the plane and we do need to make sure none of the bodies left some disease around. I'll volunteer to start cleaning."

"Then we should look for everything we could possibly use like pots and pans, silverware or anything other items for eating or cooking food. We'll take them to the shelter. Usually, in first class they have real dishes instead of paper plates. Let's look for them. Anything that's removable whether we think we can use it or not, we should take down and put on the shelves that you folks so thoughtfully provided for us.

"We need to see what's in the overhead storage and see if we could use any of the things in the small carry on cases. But first, we should let everyone chose their bags before we open any of them." Eric knew that it wouldn't be right to use the bags of the survivors. They had a right to their own belongings and it'd be up to them if they wanted to share the contents or not.

Dennis and Jim went into the airplane and opened all the doors. Then they threw the bags down to Eric and he made a place for them inside the shelter. After everyone had selected their bag, they could go through the others. But he did want to wait until they really needed something. If they were rescued tomorrow the relatives of the people who died might want the things that belonged to the deceased. But if there were some life saving items in the bags, he felt it would be okay to use them.

Dennis and Jim found some pots and pans that could be used if they made a fire. They brought them down along with the plates and dishes they found in the first class area. "Eric, we all have suitcases that we shipped. I know they are in water, but if there were someway to get them out, it would be nice for each of us to have a change of clothing."

"I thought about that. Why don't we wait one more day and then see if our sharp rocks might cut through the plane. See that dent that almost looks as though it had broken through? I bet that would be a good place to start," Dennis suggested pointing at the dent.

"What we need to do is to get some poles and rocks and build a walkway out to the plane so we don't have to get our shoes and feet wet every time we want to get into the plane," Jim declared.

"You're right. Why don't we work on that next? It's past noon. I wanted to wait and eat a little later so we can forget about the morning burial task. As soon as the gals return, we'll eat." Eric thought he heard them coming through the trees so he started dishing out the food. He hoped they found something. He was pretty sure that Leslie would since she had survival training.

"Hey everyone just see what we found: berries, roots, salad makings, all kinds of things," Bethany exclaimed. "And one of the prize vegetables we found is the wild onions. They will flavor a lot of things. I can't believe that we found them. They are strong but I promise not to use too much in the dishes. If we're stuck here, there's plenty to eat out in the woods. Just give me a pan and I'll make us some soup for dinner."

Bethany and Leslie were holding out a bunch of food for the group to see. Both girls had a smile on their faces. They wouldn't starve if they were stuck here for a few days or even if they weren't rescued for a few months. The two young women knew exactly where they could find more food.

"Well that means we have to make a fire place. Do I have any volunteers?" Eric asked and almost all of the hands went up. Everyone went in search of some rocks and it wasn't long before the fireplace was constructed.

"Now I need some pots or pans and something to fry food on," Bethany requested as she looked around.

Dennis showed her the pans they had found in the plane and Bethany smiled. This was going to be fun. If they just pretended that they were on a camping trip and forgot about the rest of the people who didn't survive, this could turn out to be a good time. It was interesting learning from Leslie all the different things that were edible. They could actually eat them raw, but Bethany decided that a warm bowl of soup would taste better than something cold.

Peter took the plastic that Eric had found and headed for the little house outback to make it a little nicer for the ladies. He, himself, wouldn't mind if it was scratchy as far as that was concerned. It was good that they'd found a type of hole they could build the structure over. With no shovel, one had to get inventive.

Peter was used to outhouses since his parents did so much camping. But he bet his bottom dollar that it was something new for the rest of the survivors. He knew the girls wrinkled up their noses every time they had to go in that little building. He just smiled. If they were there much longer without getting rescued he bet they'd get used to it sooner or later.

When they were building the outhouse, Leslie gave them strict instructions that they couldn't build it close to the stream of water nor above it. She didn't want her spring to be contaminated.

They looked at her and smiled. That did make sense so they were careful to go east a ways and then build it and make sure is didn't drain into Leslie's stream as they had named it.

Jim thought it was pretty good to have someone who could find water so easy. He had done some camping but he would have no idea where one might find water. Little by little they were building a home in case they were stuck there longer than a day or two. He definitely believed that it was a good idea to prepare for a long time on the island. For one thing, the projects that Eric suggested gave everyone something to do instead of sitting around griping because the rescue team hadn't come.

CHAPTER 5

The Rabbits

That evening they all sat around the fire place and ate the soup that Bethany had made. The roots tasted a little like potatoes would. Leslie had found some herbs for the cook. They all admitted that it was pretty tasty and came back for seconds. It was their first meal that was not airline rations and it was a nice change, Eric thought.

"Too bad we don't have some marshmallows or some hot dogs to roast over this nice fire. Does anyone have any suggestions for something to roast?" asked Bethany.

"Sure, remember those rabbits that we saw today when we gathered the food. I think this place in inundated with the little creatures. They'd be good to roast over that fire. Anyone here good with arrows or sling shot or some make shift weapon that we could use to get a rabbit?" Leslie looked around hoping maybe there was an archer in the bunch but no hands went up.

"I suggest we set a trap. Put some food in it and when the rabbit goes inside and hits the stick the door will close and lock it in. I'll make a trap and you gals furnish me with some of that salad stuff to attract the rabbit." Peter started right to work on his trap. When it was finished he took it a considerable distance from the camp so the rabbits wouldn't be afraid to come near it. Tomorrow he'd check it and see if it worked as he hoped. There did seem to be plenty of rabbits on the island.

Eric gathered the people around him once more. "You know that it's going to get cold one of these days if we aren't rescued first. We do need to start working on getting the luggage out of the luggage compartment. The suitcases are probably floating in water. We don't know what could be in that luggage compartment or in the suitcases that might help us through the next few weeks or through winter if we are forced to stay here."

"That's an excellent idea, Eric. Now that we have a fire place and know we can find food in the forest, we should work on that luggage compartment. I still think those rocks we sharpened would cut through that dented spot on the plane. It looks like it is almost through there now. That will be tomorrow's project for several of us," Peter suggested and was glad to see several of the people nod their heads in agreement.

Early the next morning, Bethany and Leslie started working on breakfast. They had found some bird eggs and decided to make some scrambled eggs with some of the greenery that they found. Bethany added some herbs to it. The men exclaimed that it was a delicious breakfast. No one was going to complain as they knew this was what they were going to live on until someone came to rescue them.

After the meal, Eric noticed that most of the men went right to work on cutting the luggage compartment. Once they got a big enough hole, they could float some of the suitcases out through the hole. The rest of them carried rocks and fallen tree limbs and worked on making a path to the plane that would relieve them from walking in the water. It wasn't long before the bridge-path was made and the men standing in the water stepped on it making sure it would hold their weight.

"That's much better," Eric exclaimed. "At least now I don't have to shiver while I'm working. That water wasn't exactly warm. Now how are you men doing as far as cutting a hole in the luggage department? I've not even made a dent over here."

"Well, that spot where the plane was dented is almost through. Another five minutes and it will be. Then perhaps we can make a hole to slip a pole in and put some pressure on it. We should probably pound the sharp rock with another rock to weaken the area around the hole that we want to make. We need to make it big enough for a suitcase to come through it," suggested Peter.

Eric noted how hard Peter had been working. Well that was good. He wasn't sure if everything would be soaked in the suitcases or if some of them were air tight. But he was quite sure there would be some equipment that they could use. Eric stepped back and watched. There was no sense in him continuing to try to cut through the outside of the airplane since Peter had almost accomplished the task. He couldn't even make a dent in the plane. It was good that the crash caused a crease in the exterior of the plane so that they could make a hole.

After the hole was finished, Peter pounded some holes around the area to make it give a little more. Then the men put all the pressure they could on the pole. It took every one of them to push on it before they finally heard some creaking noise. The hole to the luggage compartment was giving way to a big hole. It was filled with water, but none the less they could reach in and slowly get the luggage out.

It appeared that it was going to take several days to get everything out as someone would have to step inside and hold their breath while floating the suitcases out through the hole. If only there was a way to get the water out of the luggage compartment. Eric thought he might throw that idea out and see if anyone came up with a good suggestion. He sure didn't have any idea.

Some of the luggage was right where they could get at it and so they started carrying as many suit cases as they could to the shore. That bridge that was created sure helped a lot and saved shoes and socks from getting soaked.

"Albert, you wouldn't have any idea how we could get the water out of that luggage compartment would you?" Eric asked him.

"Well, let me think about it. Right now if you took water out it would come right back in because there is a hole somewhere in the compartment. If we could just raise the plane up higher or if we could bring the plane closer to shore that would drain the water. Both ideas seem almost impossible unless we find something in that storage compartment that would somehow help us." Albert kept thinking. This problem solving was right down his alley.

"Anyone else have any suggestions?" Eric asked.

No one volunteered anything. Eric could tell that Albert was thinking. Albert walked into the water and went in front of the plane. "Eric, this is probably not possible, but if we could start one of the engines on this plane, we could drive it closer to shore. I doubt if any of them would work, but it's another one of those impossible ideas. We might need to do a repair job if one of the engines is at all in good shape."

"You know, Albert, it might not be impossible. We've taken a lot of the weight out of the plane. First we need to get some more of that luggage out of the compartment. That will help, although the water in there adds a lot of weight to the airplane. Would you check to see if you can start one of the airplane engines?" Eric asked.

"Let me take a look. I'll see what I can do. Since there are four engines, one of them just might be repairable." Albert walked across the bridge, climbed the ladder and stepped into the airplane. He was in there for quite some time and no one heard anything from him. Finally they heard the growl of a motor. It was growling but not turning over.

"Hey, Peter, isn't that a good sign? I'm surprised to even hear it growling. Go up and see if Albert has discovered anything," Eric suggested.

In the mean time Dennis suggested that they make a hook out of the ski pole that came floating out of the luggage compartment. With that they could reach more baggage. Dennis made the hook. Carefully they slipped it into the luggage area and slowly brought out a suitcase. It was working great.

Now that they had taken all of the suitcases that they could reach, it was time to quit since it was getting late. They had taken a short break for the small lunch they had but now they were hungry.

"Have the two ladies returned yet and did they find anything to eat?" Dennis asked.

"Yes, we're back and we're cooking your dinner. You just have to be a little patient. We checked your rabbit cage, Peter, and you did catch one. Leslie actually killed it, skinned it and we are now cooking it for dinner. We put some more bait in there to see if we could catch one for tomorrow. We also have some vegetables to go along with the roasted rabbit." Bethany knew that the men would be good and hungry as they had worked hard all day.

The men worked on their project for another half hour and quit for the day. They had a lot of luggage to go through but that could always wait. They had retrieved luggage that belonged to the ladies and one suitcase that belonged to Jim. These were set aside for the owners to go through.

If the two girls didn't have to go find food tomorrow then they could go through the suitcases. That would be a good job for them. But food was more important and they were doing a good job finding it. Eric remembered that there was still a little food left from the airplane but he didn't want to use that until they just had to. They were mostly health bars and juices along with some pretzels.

The men really enjoyed the rabbit. "Bethany, you really are a good cook. This rabbit is delicious. How did you kill it and skin it?" asked Dennis.

"Leslie just simply hit it on the head in the right place. Then we found a rock that looked almost as sharp as a knife. She skinned it with that. You can bet we kept that knife to use on vegetables and on the rabbit we are going to catch tomorrow. I thought we would have rabbit stew tomorrow if no one has any objections," Bethany remarked.

No objections were heard.

"Boy, this is some meal," Jim stated. "That meat is so good I sure hope you do catch another rabbit tomorrow. That was just plain good eating and the salad tastes good as well."

"I agree," Peter said.

"Bethany, you're one great cook," Albert remarked. "I could eat another piece of roasted rabbit tomorrow. But rabbit stew also sounds good. It's just nice to know that we can have a little meat in our diet. You two ladies are doing a great job feeding us."

"I have to agree with the others," Eric remarked. "Bethany and Leslie, you're doing a good job in finding food for us. I don't know what herbs you put on that rabbit, but they had to be good ones. It tasted great. Perhaps there are other animals around here that we could look for and have a change of diet. Keep your eyes open, everyone and let us know if you see any animals. If we do, we'll figure out some way to catch them."

"There has to be more than just rabbits on this island," Jim remarked. "We'll find some sooner or later."

CHAPTER 6

Getting Acquainted

That evening it was a tired crew that sat around the fire place and talked. Each night they learned a little about each other. Eric decided that tonight, each person ought to tell why they took this particular airplane ride and what their destination was.

"It's too bad that we don't have a musical instrument so that when we sit around the fire, we could enjoy some music. That's what we do when we go camping. My father used to bring his guitar and we'd have a sing along," Bethany remarked.

"Well how about this," Jim questioned as he took his harmonica out of his pocket and played a little tune on it.

"Hey, that's great. Play some more," Leslie requested.

Everyone agreed and listened to the pleasant music. Finally Jim put the harmonica away.

Eric decided that he'd be the first one to tell why he took the trip. "Thanks for the music, Jim. Now let's all get a little more acquainted and tell each other what we do for a living. I worked for my dad in his factory. He keeps saying he's going to retire one day and it will all be mine, but I know him. He loves the work he does. So he sent me overseas to see about some equipment that would make our job a lot easier. So that's why I took this flight. I was supposed to stay one week and come back. I think I missed the deadline."

Leslie spoke up next. "Every year I meet some friends overseas and we take off and go into the wilderness and live just as we're living here. That's one reason this doesn't bother me any. I'm used to it. We do it every year. I'm sure that all my friends who meet at our designated place are wondering what happened to me. I told them I'd be there and what flight I was taking. They probably think I'm buried in the ocean and they'll never see me again."

Leslie hesitated a minute when she thought about it and then continued. "But I did have a job at one time. A friend of mine and I decided we wanted to be flight attendants for the summer vacation when we were in college. We just did it for an adventure, something to do but it turned out to be fun."

"You go every year and hike and try to survive in the wilderness like we're doing now?" Jim asked. "Really! You must like roughing it. No wonder you're so good at finding food. I think the good Lord put you in here with us as we sure need you. We wouldn't be eating half so well if it weren't for you."

Leslie only smiled. She had no comment to make on what Jim said. She had never thought one way or the other about God but watching Bethany and talking to her made her wonder if…

Peter decided it was his turn to speak up. "Well, to tell the truth, I was going on a vacation, that's all. I had three weeks saved up and I thought I'd tour Europe. I just hope I have a job left when I get back."

"Oh, they always need newspaper boys," laughed Albert. Peter and Albert had talked a lot and Peter had told him that he was a newspaper reporter and also that he had been a cook in a restaurant.

"I'm not a newspaper boy now, I just used to be. I'm a newspaper reporter, Albert. I write some of that stuff you read in your paper every morning. I was sent overseas to find out about a particular story that the editor wanted cleared up. Some of the facts were not as they should be. He wanted me to rewrite the story," Peter stated.

"And," Albert said without finishing.

"Yes, Albert, I do put a recipe in the paper now and then. It wasn't my idea but as soon as the editor knew that I once worked in a restaurant, he strongly and I mean strongly suggested I fill that corner so I did. Albert, I'm not a newspaper boy now!" Although Peter knew that Albert was teasing, he liked to see people laugh at Albert's comment and they did just that.

Albert did all he could do to keep from laughing. If he'd been Peter he wouldn't have confessed that he wrote out recipes but somehow he knew Peter did it to give everyone a good laugh even if it was at his own expense.

"You're going to have quite a story to write when you get back, Peter. Are you going to let us read it first?" Eric asked with a grin.

"I doubt it. You'd all want to change everything I put in it. I want to come out as the hero and I'm sure each one of you probably would think that you were the hero when I know that I was."

"Would you listen to that," Dennis quipped. "If that article doesn't say that we're all heroes I'm going to come looking for you."

"You just have to wait until the article comes out. It could be some time. We have to get home first," Peter laughed. It certainly didn't hurt to have a few laughs around the fire in the evenings. It did build up the moral of the camp. What the people didn't realize was that Peter was taking pictures with his digital camera. He wanted a great news story full of actual pictures of the shelter, airplane, people and all. He even went back and filmed the grave which was rather sad but if he were to do a complete story that would have to be included.

"Is that why you've been sneaking around and taking snapshots of everyone," Leslie remarked in a sarcastic manner.

"You mean you caught me. Here I thought I was being so careful. Yes, when I get through, the pictures will hit the newspapers all over the country and my book will be full of the pictures I have taken as well. You'll all be famous because of me and my talent," Peter declared with a smile.

"Oh, yes, of course," Dennis declared.

"Can we see the pictures?" Bethany asked.

"One of these evenings we shall just do that," Peter promised.

Albert decided he would be next. "I'm an engineer. I work for a big company and they sent me overseas to talk with some of the engineers there about a project we're working on together." He didn't tell the whole truth about his position. He thought it was better to just let them know he was an engineer.

"What's the project about?" Dennis asked.

"Well, you see, it's like this. It's not for publication just yet. I'd be in deep water if I talked about it. Not that we're all almost in deep water to begin with. But it's an exciting occupation and I even enjoy going to work each day. I especially like it because I'm one of the supervisors."

"That's great, Albert. Since we have to work, we might as well enjoy it. Now as for me, "Dennis stated, "I was just going on vacation. Just a month's vacation since I hadn't taken one for two years. There was so much work to do that I couldn't get away. I work for a firm that installs heating equipment in homes.

"Sometimes it keeps me so busy but the boss finally had pity on me and told me to take a vacation and I didn't ask him if he could do without me. I just said I would do that. I could say this is some vacation, but you know, it hasn't been that bad once we got over the first initial problems. If it wasn't for all the fatalities in the crash, this would be a great experience."

"Do you like what you do, Dennis?" Leslie asked.

"Yes, I do. You meet a lot of people especially the new owner of the homes you install the equipment and I like that. And there are several different heating systems and seems there are a lot of options to choose from when it comes to selecting heating equipment for your home. I've even had people invite me back to have dinner with them. I made some great friends over the years."

Bethany spoke up next. "I won a contest and that's how I was able to take this trip. I was going to visit some relatives over in Ireland. My parents were killed in an automobile accident about six months ago. I had a hard time adjusting to it but an aunt welcomed me into her home. I had just finished college and was about to apply for a job and that happened. I had a hard time deciding what I wanted to be and kept changing my courses. I qualify to be a teacher and I may still do that. But what I'd really like to be is a librarian. I love books and sure have missed them although we've kept pretty busy without having something to read besides the airline magazines. But I do love to read good books."

"That's good," Peter interrupted. "When I write my book about our experience I know of at least one person who will read it."

Bethany ignored him and went on with what she intended to say. "My parents were so proud that I was going to be a teacher. And I may still do that. I'm not in any hurry. My aunt thought it would be good for me to visit my relatives in Ireland. They came to America one time and we had a blast with them. So I thought it would do me good to take the trip."

"I'm sorry about your parents, Bethany," Eric remarked. That was probably the reason that Bethany was so quiet. "If we're on this island too long, we shall have to start a school and you'd be the teacher."

Bethany laughed. "And just what do you think I could teach all of you? I was going to be a kindergarten or first grade teacher. I think you've all passed those grades already."

"If you were the teacher, I know five men that would come to the class just to see the beautiful teacher every day," Peter exclaimed and winked at Albert.

"I'd be right there too," Albert agreed.

"Well, we've heard from everyone except for Jim. What are you doing on this trip?" Eric asked.

"Taking an airplane ride that didn't come out too good," he answered.

"You were just on vacation?" Eric asked.

"Not exactly, but I was unfortunate enough to get on this airplane. Not that it has been too bad except for the fatalities. We sure have learned a lot about how to survive in the wilderness. It's been a great time working with all of you. I have a feeling that we'll all get back home one of these days. All the efforts we've made are going to pay off. You just wait and see and try to be patient."

"What do you do for a living," Eric asked knowing that Jim completely avoided the subject. He didn't appear to want to tell them what his occupation was. Eric couldn't help wondering why.

"I think I'll just let you think about it. If I tell you, I may lose you all as my friends and I don't want to do that," Jim remarked smiling a mischievous grin. He wasn't sure he wanted them to know what he did for a living. He knew that some of them wouldn't like it at all.

"Now what occupation could you have that would make us stay away from you. Come on, tell us," Dennis demanded.

"Maybe sometime later I will, but not just now. Tonight we discovered that we had a teacher, a manufacturer, an engineer, a news paper boy..."

"A newspaper reporter if you will," snapped Peter.

"Oh, yes, that's right," Jim replied. "And let's see we have a hiker, but our hiker didn't give us her occupation. What do you do for a living, Leslie?"

"I'm ashamed to tell you that I haven't started any job as yet except for that few months my friend and I were flight attendants. I finished college as my parents wanted me to but I just took some business courses. I'm one of those daughters from the filthy rich people who don't have to work. But I do plan on going to work in two or three more years or so. I just wanted to live a little first. I wouldn't mind just being a housewife one day. You see I don't have all that much ambition except when it comes to hiking. Then I have all the ambition in the world."

"You want to be a house wife and you said you're filthy rich. Okay, fellows, here's your chance to marry a rich gal," Dennis quipped and doubled up laughing.

"I didn't say I was ready to marry yet. Come around in about three years and I'll think about it," Leslie replied and laughed with them.

Bethany looked at Jim. "Now it's your turn to tell us what you do," she stated as sweetly as she could. She was curious as to what he could do for an occupation that he didn't want to tell them.

"If you guess what it is, I'll tell you. Otherwise I'm going to wait until we're on our way home," Jim stated definitely.

"You must be a crook or bank robber. No wonder you don't want to tell us," Dennis remarked.

"Well, I haven't tried that occupation but maybe I will sometime," Jim answered and grinned.

"I'd say you were the supervisor in some company. You're too quiet and you're always studying people. Am I right?" Eric questioned.

"Well, I do own my own business and so therefore I'm the boss. You got that right. That will be one point for Eric."

"Are you a minister?" Albert asked. That was one person some people avoided and especially him. He kept clear of any preacher. He was tired of hearing what they had to say about sin.

"No, but that wouldn't be a bad occupation. But I'm not a minister."

"Do people come to you for advice?" Leslie asked.

"Yes, they usually do if they want to do business with me. However some people already have their mind up and know exactly what they want. But most people ask my advice."

"But you don't advise them about anything else. You're not a psychiatrist are you?" Dennis questioned.

"No, and if I was I sure wouldn't want to psychoanalyze this group." Jim laughed and looked at the group of people who looked so puzzled. He really didn't want them to know what he did for a living. He knew it would put a distance between him and some of them. People just didn't understand why someone would choose an occupation such as he had chosen. It was a calling he believed. He did have lots of chances to do some witnessing while working at his profession.

"Well, friends, it's getting late. We have visited a little longer than usual. Why don't we call it a night," Eric suggested. "Perhaps while we're sleeping we might come up with what Jim does for a living. I sure can't think of any occupation that would ostracize him from the rest of us."

"I think I know what he does," Leslie remarked with a smile.

"What?" Albert asked.

"I'm not telling. You'll just have to figure it out yourself," she stated.

"Now I'm curious," Bethany remarked. "Won't you give us a hint?"

"No, but if you keep thinking about it, you'll come up with his occupation. The thing is that Jim doesn't look like someone who would have that occupation," Leslie commented. "You would picture someone totally different. He's also very young to be in that occupation."

"Are you sure you know what I do?" Jim asked.

"Pretty sure." She walked over to Jim and whispered in his ear.

"You're right. Now you know why I didn't want to tell everyone," Jim explained to Leslie.

"Yes I do. And I think I'll keep my distance from you," she stated sarcastically and everyone laughed.

"See, that's what I said. Now that Leslie knows, she doesn't want to be my friend," Jim remarked sadly.

Leslie came over and put her hand on his shoulder. "I hope you didn't take me serious. I'm still your friend. I was only kidding."

"I know. You're too smart a gal to let something like my occupation bother you," he replied smiling at her. He liked this gal. She was smart and a lot of fun.

"Actually, I find your occupation rather interesting. If you allow me, when we get back I'd like to come and visit you. I'd like to work with you for at least one day. This sort of thing always fascinated me. There's so much to it. I know that most people shy away from that occupation, but they shouldn't."

"You're a brave lady, Leslie. I personally invite you to come and see me when we get back. I do mean when and not if. I know that we shall return to the good old United States and it won't be too long before we do. I think this little escapade has done a lot for each of us. I know it has done a lot for me. I believe that I've made some friends that will last a lifetime, Jim remarked and smiled, "that's until they discover my occupation."

Whatever occupation can that man have? No one but Leslie could even come close to guessing. Eric knew this would keep him awake wondering about it.

With that the group headed for bed.

Eric lay in his bed doing his best to think of what occupation Jim had. It rather bugged him that he couldn't guess. Usually he was pretty good at figuring out people and what they did. He could size them up and know their likes and dislikes but not Jim. He was a little too quiet for him to figure out.

But he sure fit in with the group and was always helpful in any project that needed to be accomplished. Jim worked willingly without complaint. He was a good man even if he did have a strange occupation.

CHAPTER 7

Checking the Landing Gear

Every day Albert and Peter worked on the one airplane engine that had almost turned over. They tore a lot of the metal away from the front of the plane. They were so busy that when lunch time came they had to be called to come and eat. Both of them felt that they were making progress in getting the motor to work and they'd almost rather work on that than take a break and eat but they knew they had to eat.

Jim and Dennis were working at making a bigger hook connecting the two ski poles together with vines. They were able to get a few more of the suitcases and other paraphernalia out of the luggage compartment, but they could tell that there was much more in there that needed to come out.

Leslie and Bethany were off gathering food. Bethany kept thinking about what they would do if they happened to have to stay through winter. "Leslie, if we're here all winter, what will we do? We can't gather food then. I wonder if we should start drying food and start storing a few things here and there for winter. I know that it's only July and we have several months, but what if…?"

"I've thought of that too but I just have a feeling we aren't going to be here that long. But it sure wouldn't hurt anything to gather extra and put it in some type of storage bag. There are so many berries and these can be dried and a little of our spring water added to it and we'd have a nutritious drink. While the berries are on, I think we should do that. There is no way we can eat all these delicious delicacies before they spoil."

"Couldn't we grind some of those roots and turn them into flour. However, we need something to grind with," Leslie stated.

"You know, Albert might have some good ideas on that. Then of course they just might find something on the plane or in luggage from which we could make a grinder. We'll ask when we get back and also, I think we should share our idea with the others. It will only be a little more work to save a few things for winter just in case."

Yes, she'd ask Albert when they returned, thought Bethany. It seemed to help Albert when you asked his advice. If he was an engineer, then he should be able to come up with something for a grinder.

"Now that we have our salad material, let's check and see if we have another rabbit. That sure was good tasting last night after not having any good meat for so long," Leslie commented.

"Oh, I agree. I hope we have another one."

They walked to the rabbit trap and there was another rabbit. Leslie quickly killed and skinned the rabbit. "I wonder if we should start keeping the skins. Can you think of something that we could use them for? Wouldn't it make the shelter warmer if we put the skins on the outside of the shelter?"

"I think it would make it warmer," Bethany answered.

"Let's take the skins back and ask the men. It seems like a good idea to me. We hope we don't have to face the winter here but we just don't know. For one thing, there are no airplanes flying over head. That's the part that worries me," Leslie confessed. "We should be able to hear airplanes if we were on the route to Europe. But if the pilot turned off course to try to land close to an island, then we probably wouldn't hear any airplanes or see any ships."

"I know. That bothers me too. It's too quiet to be in the path of traffic to Europe. But somehow, God will find a way to have us rescued. In the meantime, none of us are hurting and we are actually having a nice time camping."

"Yes, I agree. It's a good group of people and I'm enjoying myself." Leslie agreed but didn't comment on God's ability to find a way to rescue them.

"I wonder if there are any other types of animals we might be able to catch," Bethany remarked. "It would be good to find a deer, but what would we kill it with. Unless someone was really good at aiming a big rock at it and knocking it out, then we could kill it. But we haven't seen any deer or deer tracks. There has to be more than just rabbits on this island. We'll get the fellows to look out for some other animals."

When they had plenty of berries and salad mixings along with the roots and the rabbit, they returned to their camp. The men were all hungry so they began a quick lunch.

While they were eating, Leslie asked the men what they thought about keeping the rabbit skins and attaching them to the shelter to keep it warmer in case we spend the winter here.

"I think that we ought to save the skins for now and dry them out. Let's wait a couple of months and see what happens. If we're still here then, we should definitely attach all the rabbit skins we have to the shelter," Eric suggested.

Everyone was in agreement. They didn't like to think of living through a winter in this place. They had no idea where they were and if the winters were rough or warm. They'd plan for a cold winter and hoped for a warm one if they weren't rescued before the cold came.

After lunch the ladies decided to look through some of the luggage. It was mostly clothes they found. There were some jewelry, some toothpaste and cosmetics, and a variety of other items. So far nothing they could use to make a grinder.

"Albert," Bethany called.

"Yes, Bethany, what can I do for you?" When Bethany called Albert was right there to answer. It wasn't hard to see that he had a crush on the young lady. But then he wasn't the only one.

"We need a grinder to grind some of these roots into flour. Then we can make pan cakes and other things. Do you have any suggestions? We thought by looking through the luggage we just might come up with some items that might make a grinder. What do you think?"

"Bethany, I think I could fix you a grinder with something that I found on the airplane. We're working on getting the motor started and

Peter and I are hopeful that we can. We want to move it up on the land but we have to make sure we have wheels underneath to drive with. Anyway, you wait right here and I'll be back in a few minutes. It may take me a little time to fix it." Albert hurried up the steps and into the airplane.

He had noticed that the little space where the flight attendants prepared the drinks had a drink mixer. Now he would have to come up with some type of a handle but he thought he could do that. It wasn't long before he had a handle on the mixer and brought it back down to the camp.

"See if this will work. I know it isn't very big, but you could grind a few roots at a time," Albert suggested. "I'd cut the roots into little pieces first."

Bethany smiled at him. "Thank you, Albert. This is great!"

She and Leslie set everything up and gave the mixer a try. Sure enough it ground the roots into fine flour like substance. The girls were pleased. One more thing they could add to their menu to make some type of variety in the things that they'd eat. They could think of lots of ways to use that grinder.

The two ladies spent the rest of the day going through the luggage. Each person had claimed their own and put their things in their part of the shelter. The rest of the suitcases they carefully went through to see if there were anything in them to help them survive incase they were stuck on this island more than just a few more days.

They both laughed when they opened one suitcase. No water came in it and it was filled with food.

"What are you two laughing at?" Eric asked.

"We found a suitcase full of food. Someone must have thought they were going to starve wherever they were going. It's mainly health bars and things on that sort. There are some powders to make drinks. This is one big suitcase. Thank you, Lord, for this bounty," Bethany remarked.

"Amen," Leslie added.

Albert and Peter had gone back to trying to work on the engine of the airplane. It was close to starting but even if it did start and there were no wheels under it, it would do no good. They had planned on clearing all of the trees and everything in front of the plane and driving it right up on the land. Some of the men were already clearing the way in anticipating of the plane moving.

"One of us has to swim under the plane and check to see if the wheels are down and in good shape. They should be okay since the plane landed in water and came in head first. Are there any good swimmers who can hold their breath for a minute or so in order to check on the wheels?" Albert asked.

"I'm a good swimmer and I can hold my breath a pretty long time," Dennis volunteered. "I'll be glad to swim under there and check it out. Isn't one of those flashlights we found water proof? I'd need to be able to see. And didn't we find some goggles in one of the suitcases. That would help as well." Dennis looked into the suitcase where the goggles were found and dug further. Just as he thought, there was a wet suit. That was much better. Although he had a change of clothes in his suitcase, he liked the idea of the wetsuit. It wouldn't be so cold in the water.

Everyone stopped working and watched as Dennis donned the outfit and goggles and swam under the plane. Eric held his breath. He didn't want the man to get hurt and advised him to be very careful. They watched as his head went under the water. No one said a word but stared at the moving water that covered their friend's head.

Eric kept waiting for him to come back. It had to be at least a minute that he was gone. It seemed longer. He began to pace. "I think someone needs to go in a check on him," Eric suggested.

"No," Albert stated. "It has been less than a minute. I've been timing him. He told me that he could hold his breath for a good two minutes or more. He's fine. He has to have time to check the wheels out and make sure they are down and okay."

Eric didn't like the fact that it was taking so much time. Perhaps he should check on him regardless of what Albert said. He waded out a ways in the water when all at once Dennis popped his head up and drew a big breath. Everyone breathed a big sigh of relief when they saw him emerge from under the water. They gave him time to catch up on his breathing before asking questions.

"Are the wheels in good shape?" Albert asked.

"It's amazing, but they are. Nothing wrong with them at all! If you get that engine started and we clear the front of that plane, there is no reason why we couldn't drive it up on the beach. But we should make sure that we clear everything out of the way so that there's no obstruction in front of the plane. It wouldn't hurt to smooth the makeshift roadway a little to make it easier to drive the plane up on the shore." Dennis was as pleased with what he found about the wheels as the rest of the survivors were.

"We're working on that now," Eric informed him. "Do you know what it would mean to us if we could get that plane on land? Just think if they don't find us and winter comes on, we'll need to use the plane. We hope that they find us soon, but it has been over two weeks and nothing so far. I don't think they'll quit looking yet. Perhaps we should put some white cloth in the trees as a signal. Can anyone think of anything else we could do to attract their attention?"

"We could put some of that tinfoil in the trees. Someone would have to climb up there a ways and put them in the trees so that it can be seen from the middle of the ocean. We need to cut the tinfoil in strips so that it will move back and forth," Bethany suggested.

"That's a good idea. Leslie, are you ready to climb another tree," Eric asked. He hated to ask her but she seemed to be the only tree climber in the bunch and if you were going to climb up tall trees, you needed to know what you were doing.

"I'll be glad to. Bethany and I will fix the tinfoil. We don't want to use too much of it as it is so handy for other things like roasting food, but we can spare some. Do you want us to get some white shirt or something from one of the suit cases and hang that too?" Leslie asked.

"Yes, that would be good. I think this is the best tree to use for a signal," Eric suggested as he pointed to a very tall tree. "It will face the ocean and it looks as though there are plenty of limbs to help you climb up quite a ways." Eric was pleased that Leslie was so cooperative. Anything he asked her to do, she agreed. He was rather pleased that there were two nice young ladies in the survivor group.

In the meantime, the men kept working on removing all the trees and junk in front of the plane. Eric knew it was no easy task. Albert and Peter kept working on the motor. They were very hopeful although some of the others thought it might be a lost cause but kept their thoughts to themselves.

To Eric it appeared that there was something they needed to make in order to fix the motor and they were going to have to make that particular product themselves. That would not be as easy as it seemed as they didn't have any equipment to make things with except sharpened rocks. He'd always carried a pocket knife, but you weren't allowed to take one on the airplane. It sure would have come in handy.

Eric liked the cooperation that everyone was giving. Even if they were rescued in the next few days, working on projects was a lot better than sitting around doing nothing except wondering when they were going to be rescued.

Leslie was back with tinfoil and some white shirts and string. She began climbing up the tree. It was pretty tall and she figured she'd get close to the top of the tree and then tie her tinfoil and shirts so that they would wave and attract attention. It didn't take her too long to accomplish her task and she was heading back down the tree. No one may see it but then again you never knew, she thought.

"The next thing we should do is to walk up that mountain and try the cell phone. Check your phones and see if they are still powered up. It's been sometime and they may not be charged," Eric suggested.

Sure enough, the batteries in everyone's cell phone had run down. Well that wasn't going to work out so well. They should have tried climbing the mountain and using the cell phones before but no one thought about it. Now all the cell phones were useless.

"Albert, do you have any suggestions when it comes to powering up our cell phones?" asked Bethany.

"I sure do. Just let us get this engine working and you can plug one or two of them in the power outlet on the plane. That will do it. But we have to wait until the engine is running. The other thing is to look into the suitcases and see if anyone brought spare batteries for their cell phone. Sometimes people do." Albert smiled at Bethany. She seemed to have a lot of faith in him to know what to do and he liked that. Because of her the others were beginning to respect him a little more and ask for his advice. He didn't feel quite the outsider so much anymore.

"Albert, that's a good suggestion. If we had been thinking, some of us should have taken the batteries out and then we'd have some charged batteries for at least one of the cell phones. But it's too late to worry about what we didn't do. I think we had enough to worry about when we first landed. We didn't even think about having charged cell phones," Eric commented.

"You got that right," Dennis quipped. "We sure didn't know what we were going to do but we all worked together and we survived. You're all a great group of people and I'm glad that I met all of you."

"You're right, Dennis. This is a good group of people. Now back to the subject of walking up that hill. I still think that's a good idea. We need to see what is up there and see if there is anything there that we might be able to use. It's a long walk up that hill but if two of you took a lunch, I'm sure that you could make it up there and back in one day." Eric looked around to see if anyone disagreed with him.

"I know it will take most of the day but it's worth a try. Once we get the stuff cleared away from the front of the plane, perhaps Jim and I could walk up there and see what is there. It probably is more of the same as what is here, but we don't know. There could be people on the island," Dennis suggested.

"Yeah, head hunters," Albert remarked and laughed.

Eric didn't think the comment was all that funny but he didn't say anything. Albert had a different sense of humor than most people. He had to admit that the man was very intelligent as far as solving problems was concerned. He just lacked a little in social skills. He often wondered what type of childhood he had in his younger years. Right now he was glad to have Albert in the group even though he didn't appreciate him the first few days.

"You two fellows think about what you'd need to take with you. I do think you should plan it out carefully. Take some flares just in case you need them. Think over what you might run into and plan to take some type of protection."

"We'll do that, Eric. Just let us help a little more with this path to drive the airplane on to the beach and we shall be on our way. I'm a pretty good mountain climber and I think Jim is too. It certainly will be a change in what we have been doing," Dennis declared.

"I rather like the idea," Jim exclaimed. "Who knows what's up there? And a nice walk up the mountain sounds like a good change of pace!"

CHAPTER 8

Albert's Problem

Eric had some more ideas to try to attract the attention of the airplanes that might sometime fly over or the ships that could come close enough to see them. He found it strange that they heard no airplanes at all and never saw one ship. They must be on some remote island and not on the usual route to Europe. That was all that he could figure out.

The airplane must have been flying quite a while after the small aircraft rammed into it. Otherwise, they'd be right in the line where the planes go to and from Europe. The pilot must have figured he'd run into an island if he kept it going in one direction long enough. Eric remembered that the crash of the small airplane had awakened him but since they were still flying, he wasn't too worried.

Now that he thought about it, there was considerable time between the small plane crash and the plane landing. He remembered walking back to the bath room thinking everything was probably okay since the motors were still running but he knew that they were definitely way off the usual flying course to Europe.

He walked over to Bethany and put his arm on her shoulder. "Bethany, I want to ask you something," he said.

"Get your hands off of her," Albert yelled and started coming toward him. He had no right to touch her. He may be the leader, but he could keep his hands to himself. Albert turned red with anger.

Eric slowly removed his hand. He hadn't thought a thing about it and he sure didn't want to upset Albert. For some reason, the man thought that he owned Bethany. He had to admit that Bethany was very careful with Albert.

Bethany stepped between Albert and Eric. "Please, Albert, don't. He didn't mean anything by putting his hand on my shoulder. He was just getting my attention." She looked at Albert and smiled.

Albert backed off and walked into the woods.

"I'm going after him," Bethany announced and hurried to catch up with him. She didn't want him upset. He was just beginning to fit in with them and she hated the fact that this incident happened to upset him. Albert was a very intelligent man and they needed his cooperation. He was very nice to anyone who was nice to him.

Bethany knew that Albert and Eric didn't get along from the very beginning and she wondered why. Anyone could get along with Eric. He was so easy going. Now Albert was just a little different. He had a chip on his shoulder just waiting for some one to knock it off. For some reason, he had taken a dislike to Eric.

"Albert, I want to walk with you. Is that all right," Bethany asked.

"I always like your company, Bethany. I'm sorry that I acted so stupid. Eric just drives me up a wall and to see him put his hand on your shoulder... Well, I just couldn't take it. He's so much like my father."

"Tell me about your father," Bethany requested. "How is he like Eric?"

"Well, Eric thinks he knows everything just like my dad. You can't argue with my father because he's always right. He's always pretty easy going if you don't cross him. I crossed him one time and that was it."

"How did you cross him," Bethany asked.

"Well, my parents were paying for my university expenses. They wanted me to be either a doctor or a lawyer. I certainly didn't want to be a doctor. I had no interest in that at all. I just couldn't even imagine cutting someone open or listening to someone complain about all their pains and all that stuff doctors have to listen to. I just couldn't bare the idea and told my parents that.

"So then they decided I'd be a lawyer. I wasn't the least interested in being a lawyer either but that was the only way they'd pay the expenses for my education. I told them that I wanted to be an engineer, but they didn't think that was an important enough occupation for the only son of Herbert Desmond."

"That's too bad they wouldn't listen to you. An engineer is a very good occupation. So did you not go to college?" Bethany asked.

"Yes, I went to college. I took one course each year to be a lawyer but I took lots of courses to be an engineer. My folks didn't realize that I was doing that. The lawyer courses were so boring, I couldn't stand them. I did just enough to get by. When I was almost through my third year of college, they somehow found out what I was doing. I think they went through my papers at home."

"That's too bad. It's hard for me to think of parents that would force their son into something he didn't want to do. Do you have any idea why they insisted on you being either a doctor or lawyer?"

"Yes, that's what my father wanted to be but his parents were poor and he couldn't go to college. He wanted to be a doctor. He became a medic through courses at the junior college when he was older. He wanted us to start calling him doctor. I refused. But anyway, that was the end of me getting any financial help from them. If I wasn't going to be a lawyer, they weren't going to help me. It was as simple at that."

"So what did you do?" she asked.

"I finished the third year, but I had no money to pay for the fourth so I didn't get my degree. I was so close. I just picked up a job that was as near to engineering as any but I couldn't raise enough money to finish my course. But the supervisor really liked my work and he agreed to pay for my education if I'd go to school at night. Sometimes I had to take a class in the day time, but it all worked out. I became an engineer but I never let my parents know. I may tell them someday, but I wanted them to find out when they read in the newspaper about some project that I'm heading up."

Albert hesitated for a minute. He never told anyone else about this but Bethany seemed to be able to drag things out of him. "I go see my parents once in a great while. I visit on Christmas. I see my mother on Mother's Day but that's about it. Each time I go, I hear my dad say what a failure I am. That gets real old real quick, Bethany. I suppose I should have told them that I completed my course and became an engineer and had a real good job, but I never did."

Bethany had a hard time accepting his story. She knew he was telling the truth, but it was hard to think of parents as being as stubborn as Albert's parents were. Just because his dad couldn't be the doctor he wanted to be, he was trying to force his son into becoming something he didn't want to be.

"Bethany, I know this isn't the time or place and I shouldn't say anything, but I really like you. In fact, I love you."

Bethany answered slowly. "Albert, I'm a Christian. I don't know if you know anything about Christianity or not. But I'd only date a Christian man." She looked him right into the face.

"My parents are Christians. And I used to be but I was so disgusted because they wouldn't pay for my college just because I didn't become a lawyer. I tried hard to talk to them but they wouldn't listen. I just walked out and didn't come back for a long time. But I used to go to church, Bethany. I just got bitter," Albert confessed.

"Don't you miss some things about church?"

"Sometimes, but I kept up my bitterness to cover it up. I've felt more in tune with God since I've been on this island than I have in a long time. Some of those men are real Christians and I rather envy them."

"You know what you have to do, don't you?" Bethany said slowly and sweetly.

"I just need a little more time. To tell the truth, I've been thinking about it," Albert confessed.

Bethany decided not to ask any more questions. She felt much better about Albert knowing that at one time he was a Christian and knew all about salvation. She just couldn't understand his parents. And they were Christians. But then, as she has always been told and knew, Christians were not perfect, they were just forgiven.

The two walked back to camp. "Thanks for coming after me and letting me talk with you about my past. It really helped me." Albert wanted to pick up her hand, but he knew that a romance during this time on the island wasn't a good thing. He'd wait and he hoped that Bethany would take a walk with him again.

When they arrived in camp, everyone was doing some type of job. Bethany knew it was time to start their dinner, but before she could do anything, Leslie took a rock and hit a piece of tin to get everyone's attention.

She made an announcement that no one wanted to hear. "Friends we are out of the toilet paper that was on the airplane. Now we have to use the magazine in the airplane instead of toilet paper. I advise you to go easy on the magazine paper. When that's all gone, we'll have to use cloth. We can tear up some of the clothes in the suitcases and use that. I was hoping the airplane had more toilet paper but it doesn't. There are a few tissues around but they are limited."

"Use magazine paper? Ugh! That's gross, Leslie. That would be rough." Bethany didn't like the sound of that at all.

"The magazine pages are a lot better than leaves. And that would be an option but cloth is a lot better." Leslie looked around at the bunch. She was amused at her new friends. Some were rather embarrassed and others were just plain stunned. How could they think that the toilet paper in the airplane would last forever? They were lucky that it lasted this long. She'd been watching the supply and knew they were down to the last bit of paper.

"Leslie is right," Eric stated. "We just make the best of what we have. When you ladies have time, you might start ripping up some of the clothes in the suitcases that can be torn easily. We might as well be prepared. The magazines aren't going to last but a week or so. I know most of you have been reading them so you better hurry up and finish as they now have another purpose."

"Well, if that isn't the limit. One more thing I've learned about roughing it—magazine tissues and cloth tissues. Amazing," Dennis quipped with a grin. He hadn't even thought of this as a problem. Good old Leslie, when it came to camping in the rough, she had an answer for everything.

Peter had listened to everything but said nothing. He was uncomfortable with the whole conversation but understood that it was something that had to be discussed. At least they had a few options. He'd go along with the cloth and the magazines but preferred not to think about the leaves.

Jim was another one who said nothing. He had his time of roughing it and knew that once they got used to something, they'd think it was pretty much normal. Actually he began to think this was a pretty good group of people. No one complained about the food but ate it and praised Bethany's cooking almost every meal. They sure could have been a lot more ornery about it all. Jim was impressed with his new friends.

He never heard one complaint about the bed they slept on either. There were a lot of things this group of people could have complained about, but they didn't. He sure could have been stranded with a lot worse people than what he had. Yes, they were a pretty good group.

That evening, Eric thought about what Leslie had said and about the reaction of the group. It was almost funny. He had camped enough to know that you had to improvise when you didn't have what you needed. So far they had everything they had to have to survive. There were certainly enough clothes to tear up to make toilet tissues from them. What would be the next interesting thing that would happen, he wondered.

He was sleeping pretty close to the partition that divided the girls' bedroom from the men's. He could hear Bethany whisper to Leslie.

"Did you really use leaves? Ugh! I can't even imagine."

Eric did all he could do to keep from laughing.

CHAPTER 9

The Top of the Mountain

The next morning was Sunday morning. Eric wanted to try an experiment but he didn't know how it would go over. They all ate the good breakfast that Bethany and Leslie had prepared for each of them. Then Eric casually made a suggestion.

"Since it is Sunday, I wonder if you'd allow me to hold a very short service to honor God. Jim could play the harmonica and we could sing along with a hymn or two. Jim, play *The Old Rugged Cross* and we'll sing that song. I think almost everyone knows that hymn." Eric didn't give any one a chance to object. He was pretty sure that most of the survivors would go along with it if they believed or not.

Eric was right. Everyone including Albert sang along with Jim's harmonica. When that was over, Eric read a scripture out of his little new testament he always carried with him. Then he prayed. After the prayer, he exclaimed, "Church service is over."

Bethany was the first one to say anything. "Thanks, Eric. I sure do miss church. Perhaps we can do that every Sunday if no one objects. And maybe we can sing a few more songs next time."

No one was about to object to anything that Bethany suggested. One look at the beautiful girl and they all succumbed to her wishes. Albert even smiled. If it pleased Bethany, he'd go along with it.

It took the rest of the week to clear the stuff from the front of the plane. Jim and Dennis made the makeshift road very smooth for the airplane to drive on. Now if only Albert and Peter could get that engine running that would be good. It did seem to Dennis as though it was an impossibility to achieve that goal. But the two mechanics appeared to think that in another week they should be able to accomplish the deed.

Dennis had watched the two as they worked on the airplane engine from time to time. There seemed to be so many things that needed to be repaired that it all took time. He noticed that they were actually making by hand some of the parts that were required. But before they did that they had to find the right material to make the different items that were required. At least they found tools on the airplane and that helped considerably with the engine repairs.

Dennis had to admire Peter and Albert for all their hard work. They sure knew what they were doing and were patiently making progress. At least that's what they claimed was happening and Dennis didn't doubt it.

The next morning Jim and Dennis made a decision. Since the road was made smooth for the airplane, the two decided that it was time to climb that mountain. They made themselves a quick lunch plus they took some containers of water. They might find springs along the way but the two weren't going to take any chances of going all day without water.

Eric encouraged them to take a club or something in case they ran across any aggressive wild animals. So they sharpened some rocks that would cut and attached them to their club in case they got in a fight with a wild animal.

"This type of tool worked for the Indians long ago, so it should work for you two," Eric exclaimed.

"We need one of those flares," Jim remarked.

Eric brought a flare for each of them. "Now if you light the flares, we'll assume that you're in trouble and will come after you. Otherwise we'll just wait for your return. Just be careful."

"All right that sounds like a good plan. We won't light them except if we need your help," Dennis agreed. That sounded sensible to him. He really didn't think anything could go wrong because he was used to mountain climbing. He was rather looking forward to the trip. He doubled checked to make sure they had a flashlight.

Jim and Dennis both looked at the top of the mountain. It looked a long ways up there. "Dennis, you know that when we reach the top, there may be another top and another top. We probably aren't looking at the real top of the mountain."

"Yeah, Jim, I thought about that. Never the less we need to go and see what is up there. I hope it's truly the top of the mountain. Are you ready? Let's go."

"As ready as I ever will be," Jim answered.

The two men started up the mountain. There was no trail so they had to work at making their way up. Eric told them to be sure to leave some type of markers ever so often so they didn't get lost coming back down the mountain. It was very easy to get turned around he had told them. He sure hoped they followed his suggestions.

"Don't worry, Eric. I'm an old mountain climber," Dennis professed. "This isn't my first mountain to climb and it won't be my last. I've never been disorientated on any climb as yet. We'll be fine, I promise you."

Eric and the ladies watched as the two men climbed. They watched until they could see them no more. Too many trees were in the way. Finally they came out of the trees to a bare spot but the two men were only tiny specs by now.

Eric finally went back to work. He was sorting through some of the suitcases along with Leslie and Bethany to see what they could use. It was amazing how many things they had already found that helped them in their surviving efforts. The towels, wash clothes, soap and other personal items were going to come in handy. Eric smiled when he looked at the vase that Bethany had found. She picked some wildflowers and put the vase on the table. Leave it to those two young ladies to spruce up the shelter.

In one suitcase, there was a lot of electrical equipment. That seemed strange to Eric. Why would someone bring all this equipment and how did it pass inspection. But as he looked at it, he realized that it had to be someone's suitcase that was an electrician and he was probably headed for some job to do. The more Eric looked at it the more pleased he was about the contents.

"Albert and Peter, I have found a suitcase full of electrical equipment. You two might want to take a look at it. Perhaps you could use some of these things. When you get a break come on down."

"Eric, we're coming down now. We are having trouble creating one of the parts we need. If there is something in that suitcase that'll help, we're all for it. Let's go Peter," Albert suggested.

Both men smiled when they looked at the equipment. "This man was headed for a job somewhere. He has all the equipment he needed to repair some electrical problems in some establishment. Boy can we use these. This should speed up things considerably," Albert exclaimed. "This is great."

Peter agreed with him. "Keep looking in to the other suitcases and luggage. No telling what you might find. It would be good to find some cell batteries but then we might not need them when we get that engine going. Eric, I checked on the gas and there is plenty. That's one thing we don't have to worry about. Because the plane landed in the water, not too much damage was done except where it hit head on with the trees and the hole in the luggage compartment. I think the pilots were hoping to knock the trees down and drive the plane upon the beach but the trees they ran into were just too big for the airplane."

Eric was more enthused than ever while looking through more suitcases. They still had more luggage to search through. The girls had found a good place in their shelter to store the suitcases that were worth storing. They had found certain items that they could use. There were still about ten suitcases to go through plus whatever they would get out of the luggage compartment once the plane was on dry land.

Dennis and Jim were hiking up the mountain.

Leslie and Bethany had gone after food. Each day they had found a rabbit in the trap. Bethany tried to cook it different each day. She knew there seemed to be an abundance of rabbits every where one walked. It was no wonder that one of them found the trap each day. Sometimes she fried it and sometimes she roasted it and other times she made a stew or soup from it. One time she even made sandwiches out of the cooked leftover pieces. Pancakes made good sandwiches.

It was just nice to have meat, thought Eric. And it sure was nice that Bethany was such a good cook and had so many ideas as to how to cook the rabbit. He never had rabbit pancakes before but they weren't bad eating nor were the rabbit sandwiches.

Peter and Albert seemed so interested in getting the engine started. They didn't appear to tire of their job. He had to admit that it would be quite an accomplishment for the two to get the engine going. They sure believed that they could. He hoped it wasn't just wishful thinking on their part.

Finally, Eric finished the last suitcase. He didn't find any batteries and that was disappointing. Why hadn't he thought to take the batteries out of his cell phone? But it was too late to do anything about that.

He heard the two ladies coming through the field. They were laughing and having a good time together. Although they were very opposite in nature and personality, they got along great.

"Eric," Bethany exclaimed, "look what we found—an apple tree. The apples are little and rough looking but they are apples none the less. We shall make apple sauce, apple pie, apple salad or just have plain apples to eat."

"Hey, you two are sure good scroungers. A little fruit will taste great. If there are lots of apples, perhaps we can even dry some. I see you two have a good storage of dried food in case we have to spend the winter. You're doing a great job. We hope we don't have to spend the winter here, but in case we do, we're doing everything we can to make it through. Just getting the airplane on the shore would be a good refuge from storms."

"Eric," Bethany said.

"Yes," he answered.

"Isn't it nice how everyone is cooperating in this effort? No one really seems depressed or too upset. They act almost like we're camping and trying to make the best of it. I prayed that our group would come together and work together. And that's just what they're doing. I do believe God answered my prayer."

"I know you're right, Bethany. You aren't the only one that was praying. Now, let's see what kind of lunch you can make us. It's well past lunch time but you have a smaller group to feed with Dennis and

Jim gone. Do you want to just let them have some of the energy bars and some juice and plan a bigger meal for tonight?" Eric asked.

"That's what I was thinking. Everyone is wrapped up in what they are doing. I don't know if we can pull Peter and Albert away from the plane long enough to eat," Bethany commented. "Since you found those electrical parts in that suitcase, they have worked non stop. They are like two kids with a new toy."

"I heard that," Peter yelled. "We'll be right down. We just came to a good stopping place. Boy, Eric, this is going so much faster with that equipment you found. I mean to tell you. We are positive we can fix this engine now. There's absolutely no doubt about it!"

Peter and Albert were down and out of the plane very much ready for lunch. They made no comment on the skimpy meal. They were just glad to have something to eat that would be quick so they could return to their work on the engine.

"How do you suppose Jim and Dennis are doing? Do you think they'll be back before it gets dark? That would be rather dangerous trying to walk in the dark and not too sure which direction to go?" Peter commented with a trifle worried look.

"I've been walking back and forth worrying about them and wondering if I did the right thing in encouraging them to go. But Dennis claimed that he never gets turned around and always knows which direction he's going. I sure hope that's true. I think they'll know when they reach the top how long it took and they'll try to start back allowing that much time to return."

"Did they take a flashlight with them?" Albert asked.

"I don't know. I hope they did just in case. I sure will be relieved when I see them walking into camp. I kept wondering if three or four people should go. There's safety in numbers, so they say," Eric stated.

"I wouldn't worry too much about them, Eric. Dennis is pretty good in the woods all right. He's pointed out a lot of things to me that I missed completely. I have an idea that he'll find his way back without any trouble," Peter assured him.

"I'm sure you're right," Eric agreed.

CHAPTER 10

Two Tired Hikers

The afternoon seemed to pass by slowly to Eric. It was getting dark and he began to worry about his two mountain climbers. Dennis and Jim weren't back yet and they could hear nothing rustling in the woods to indicate they were even close to camp. Eric knew it was a long ways up the mountain, but he had hoped they'd judge the distance and come back before the sun went down.

When he thought about it, he remembered that they did take a flash light but he could see no light coming down the trail toward the camp. He wasn't just sure what he should do. There wasn't much sense in sending someone after them as there was no way to know where they might be. And they certainly wouldn't be able to find any one in the pitch dark woods.

They had just finished dinner and were sitting around the fire visiting with one another. The topic was mostly about how the two men were doing and why they didn't come back before it was too dark to see.

"Albert and Peter, what do you think we should do about Dennis and Jim. It's getting dark and I'm worried. Do either of you have any suggestions?" Eric asked.

"I wouldn't worry. Jim is a mountain climber and so is Dennis. Perhaps they found something to bring back and it is just taking them longer to get here than they judged," Peter volunteered.

"No, I wouldn't worry. Both of them know what they're doing. They would have yelled or caused some type of disturbance or fired off their flares if there was any trouble. You remember they took those flares just for that purpose. Those two men know what they're doing when it comes to mountain climbing," Albert added.

"There's nothing you can do, Eric, but wait. If they're in trouble, it will have to wait till morning," Leslie stated.

"I know you're right, all of you. It's just that I wish they'd come into camp now. But they're big boys and they'll get here when they get here. But just in case, build that fire up a little higher so they can see it," Eric suggested.

Albert and Peter threw some more logs on the fire and everyone had to move back a ways to get away from the heat. One of the things they all enjoyed was sitting around the fire in the evening and relaxing. That's when they visited and rested from their day's work. There was always something to do to keep busy each day.

"While we're waiting, I was wondering if any of you know why you survived the crash. I was in the john and realized there was trouble and hung on for all I was worth. I know how Bethany survived. She had so many pillows and blankets and was packed in so tight that the crash didn't throw her around. What about you, Peter, do you know why you made it?" Eric asked.

Peter thought for a moment. "You remember the plane wasn't full. I was lying down and buckled in with two seat belts. My hands were over my head rather restricting my head from moving. I also had pillows and blankets around me. That's the only thing I can think of. I know that Dennis and Jim were doing the same thing. Since there was so much room, we each moved to empty seats and did our best to try to sleep."

"Yes, that would explain why you didn't get hurt," Eric said thoughtfully. "And Albert, do you have any idea why you made it through the crash?"

"No, I don't. I was buckled in and had a couple of pillows under my head. I had pulled my carry on case down and used it as a foot rest. I was in a pretty tight spot so it couldn't throw me around too much. I know a lot of the people didn't have their seatbelts on," Albert answered. "That one thing was probably why they were killed. As hard as the plane hit those trees, anyone not held down was going to go flying through the airplane. The bad thing was that some of them landed on people who might have survived if they hadn't been hit with a body."

"You're right, Albert. Several people died from people landing on them. Well, I was just wondering why we survived when so many didn't. When you think about it, it all makes sense. I know it was a hard crash and enough of one that if someone wasn't secured, they would go flying. And then in turn, land on someone and cause their death. Well, thank God we all made it and thank Him for all the food He has been furnishing us," Eric stated.

Albert looked at him but didn't say a word. By now he decided that he might as well just let them talk about God. Sometimes he almost believed that some power had a hand in helping them, but was it God? Was it the personal God that Bethany talked about? He didn't know and yet he did. He had gone to church as a child and teenager. Was what he learned the truth or just wishful thinking?

Everyone heard a crash and a lot of noise as if someone was dragging something through the bushes. Eric grabbed a flash light and headed toward the noise with each of the survivors following suit. Relief spread over him when he saw Dennis and Jim. What on earth were they dragging?

"Hey, does anyone want to have steak for breakfast?" asked Dennis.

"Yeah, we killed a deer and drug him all the way down here. That's why we were so late. We need to hang him up for overnight. We need to rest a bit as well. Any chance we can talk you three into hanging the deer?" asked Jim.

"Oh, might hunter, we shall be glad to hang your deer up in the tree," Peter remarked. "We'll have steak for breakfast. I can't believe it. Doesn't that sound good? Out here in the wilderness having steak for breakfast."

It wasn't long before the deer was hanging in the tree. They cut the hide off the animal and spread it out to dry. They would attach it to their shelter to make it warmer for the winter. Every little bit would help keep them warmer if...

They talked about how they could preserve the meat as they knew they couldn't eat it all in a few days. There were lots of options and different ones had their opinion as to how to make the deer last without the meat spoiling.

"When my dad went hunting, he let the deer hang for two or three days and sometimes more," Bethany remarked. "We can still cut the steaks and rib roasts and eat them. We can eat a lot of this deer in four or five days. Then we can decide what to do with the rest of it."

"If we just had some salt, we could save it that way. We probably should eat what we can and then dry it in the sun and make jerky. That's all I can think of for now," Jim suggested.

"One other thing we could try is to save all the fat from the rabbits and the deer and if we can get enough, the meat will keep if it is stored in the fat. You melt the fat and put the meat down in it. That's an old pioneer trick. So for a few days we shall collect all the fat we can just in case we have some meat left that we want to keep for a while. We'll need to heat it up so it melts and then cool it. Then we should put it in the coolest place we can find," Leslie suggested.

"Tomorrow we shall make a type of cellar to keep our perishables in. It might be good if we took Bethany and Leslie's store of food into the cellar as well. Let's plan on doing that tomorrow," Eric suggested

"Well, do you think someone could feed two tired hunters? Believe me, I'm going to have something to eat and then immediately after that, I think I'm going to bed," Dennis announced.

"Me too," Jim declared. "That was no easy task bringing that animal down the mountain and through the brush. But at least now we have a path up there. It is a crooked path, but it's a path. We did as Eric said and cut limbs so we didn't get lost. Your huge fire was a welcome sight as that kept us going in the right direction when it became dark. That was our main worry, finding our way in the dark."

"Did you see anything when you arrived at the top?" Eric asked.

"No, just more mountain tops all around. There were lots of berries and plenty of roots that Bethany likes to use when she cooks. If we get too hungry, we can always walk a ways up the mountain and gathers the roots and berries. It might be harder walking but there's plenty of food. But, no, there was nothing up there that indicated that there were other people on this island. We could see where the island ended and it is not all that big. It just has a big mountain with lost of peaks," Dennis informed them.

"Well, at least we know a little more about the island. We might do some more exploring in another direction one of these days," Eric suggested.

Bethany had dished up a plate of food for each of the two hikers. They did look very tired, she thought. She gave them each some orange juice hoping that would help them gain some of their strength back. Pulling that deer was bad enough, but to pull it down the hill when there was no trail to follow had to be really tough going.

It wasn't long before they were all asleep. As Eric was drifting off to sleep he thanked God for bringing the two men safely back to camp. Tomorrow he hoped they would get closer to fixing the engine. It had been many days since they had crashed. He had almost lost count of how many. He began to wonder if they'd get rescued or not. But one thing he knew for sure and that was that God would take care of them if they had to stay on this island the rest of their lives.

Just before he dropped off to sleep, he thought about the cellar and where to put it. It should be fairly close to the shelter just in case there was a lot of snow this winter. He couldn't ask Peter or Albert to help but the other two would make fast work of the job.

He thought about the deer. It sure was going to taste good. He remembered how good the rabbits tasted when they didn't have any meat for a few days. Now they'd have steak for breakfast and he had an idea that Bethany could make that steak taste absolutely delicious. God was good to let those men get the deer.

Then he thought about how they were able to kill a deer. They had no gun only clubs and they certainly couldn't out run a deer. How in the world did they kill it? He'd have to wait until tomorrow to find out. It really didn't matter, but he was always curious when things didn't make sense.

First thing in the morning, he would find out.

CHAPTER 11

Steaks for Breakfast

Bethany and Leslie were up a little earlier than the men. They carefully cut some of the meat off the deer. It would be good to have some steaks. Neither one of them was crazy about deer meat but this was no time to be choosey.

"What I'll do is put some herbs on the meat and that will take away a little of the wild taste. By now a change from rabbit sounds pretty good. That rabbit salad you made tasted very good last night, Bethany. You do have some creative ideas when it comes to cooking. Those dandelions do make a good salad," Leslie commented.

"I want to go back to where we were yesterday. There are a lot more things that I saw we could use. I know it's a little rough going, but we'll make it. There's another apple tree there too. Boy, those fellows sure enjoyed having an apple and an apple pie. Anything to change the diet is a good change. What really sounds good to me is some mashed potatoes but I know we aren't going to find them anywhere. We just have to mash up some roots and pretend they are potatoes and make a good gravy to go with them," Bethany remarked.

Eric was just getting out of bed. "I can smell some good meat cooking. Oh, look at that. Doesn't that look and smell great?"

"It sure does," Peter declared.

Albert was right behind him and agreed. They each took a helping and sat down by the fire and enjoyed their breakfast. "This is really good, ladies. You cooked that steak just right!" Eric exclaimed.

"I think the other two men might be a little late for breakfast. They sure looked tired when they came into camp last night," Bethany remarked.

"Oh, they were stirring when we got out of bed. It won't be long before they come around. I think the smell of steak cooking woke me up and probably did them too," Eric stated.

Sure enough, both Jim and Dennis came out of the shelter with a smile. They'd smelled the steaks and were ready for breakfast.

"This is the best breakfast I've had in ages," announced Dennis. "Good ole steaks, I'll take them any ole time. Rabbit tastes good, but there's nothing like steaks."

"I was up half the night trying to figure out how you two could kill the deer. You couldn't out run him, you didn't have a gun to shoot him, just how did you two happen to kill that deer," Eric asked.

"Do you think we should tell them, Jim, or just let them keep wondering how us might hunters killed a deer?" Dennis asked.

"If we don't tell them, Dennis, they'll pester us until we do. To tell the truth, the deer was caught in a thicket and we were able to knock him out with a big rock and then we cut his throat and he died. It wasn't that hard. Believe me, I'm no archer and I don't think Dennis is either. I think it was like the ram that was caught in the thicket for Abraham to sacrifice. God supplied it," Jim stated.

"I believe you're right, my friend," Eric agreed.

After breakfast, Peter and Albert went right to work on the engine. They told Eric that it was almost done. They attempted to start it and it did try to start but not quite. So they were encouraged in that. It sounded a lot better than the first time they tried to start it and it had barely growled then.

Eric, Dennis and Jim would first dig the cellar. With some of the things they retrieved from the luggage compartment, they would be able to dig a good size hole. All three of the men worked on it until they had a hole deep enough for food to stay cool. Then they constructed some poles to cover the hole. They needed to make sure that no animal could dig its way into the cellar. It took most of the day to make it just like they wanted it. It was deep enough to step down into.

The two ladies came back from their food gathering trip and inspected the cellar. "I heartily approve," Leslie commented.

"It's perfect. We can keep so many things in it and not worry about them going bad. This is going to be good." Bethany was so pleased.

Eric looked at the two ladies. He was pleased that they liked the cellar. It didn't take much to keep those two ladies happy.

The next day they'd go back to looking through the luggage to see what they could retrieve that might be some help. They needed to keep trying to get more things out of the luggage department and go through them. Each time they found a few items they could use for their survival.

The next day, Bethany and Leslie decided that they would go on another food gathering trip and this time they were going to go in a different direction. Although there was plenty of food where they usually went, they wanted to try something different. If there were food in one direction, it was only logical that there should be food in the opposite direction.

As they walked along, Leslie asked, "The land and area appears different in this direction than where we had been going, Bethany. Let's take our bags and go over there. Don't you think that area looks a little different than the rest of the place?" Was it just her or was it different.

"Perhaps it is just the way the sun is shining on it. But let's go. It does have a different look to it. You know what I think it looks like?" Bethany asked.

"What?"

"I think it looks like someone had worked some of the ground. I know that's not logical, but I can't help but think that's what it looks like."

Leslie thought for a moment. "You know, you're right. It does look like that. It definitely has that look. Let's go. We'll probably be disappointed when we get there but let's go see what we can find."

The two walked for quite some time before they reached their destination. "Walking through this brush makes the going pretty slow," Leslie remarked.

"I know, I think I've received a few scratches from the bushes. But they're so thick. We should have brought some cutters along so we could make a path for next time. But we're getting there slow but sure."

"Well, we're at our destination. It does look different from the other places we saw. It almost appears that someone could have lived here at one time."

"I think you're right, Leslie. I'm going over here, why don't you try over there," Bethany suggested. "There are a bunch of branches piled up and it seems rather strange way for the branches to be. It's as though someone..."

In just a moment, Leslie heard Bethany cry out and then nothing. She hurried over to where Bethany was and she wasn't there. She looked all around and then noticed the big open hole in the pile of brush that Bethany was talking about. Carefully she went to look down in the hole without getting too close. There lay Bethany motionless. Leslie turned pale.

"Bethany, are you all right?" Leslie asked.

No response came from the girl. Bethany had to be unconscious. Now, what should she do? She was too far away to yell and be heard. Why didn't she bring one of those flares that the men told them to always take just in case? She hated to leave Bethany alone, but she couldn't climb down in that hole. It was straight down.

What was that deep hole doing there anyway? It was like a trap for an animal or perhaps an enemy. It seemed a little eerie to think that someone might have lived around there before and set that trap. She had to try to wake Bethany up somehow, maybe by making a lot of noise. But then if she was really hurt, noise wouldn't wake her up.

"Bethany, wake up. Bethany," she yelled but there was no response. She didn't look as though she was dead but she definitely wasn't conscious.

Leslie made the decision to go back to the camp and get some of the men to come and help her. They needed to bring some of the rope they found in the plane and some type of bed so they could get Bethany out of there. Perhaps even a ladder. Her mind was racing as she ran toward the camp. "Oh, God, don't let her die," she prayed.

"I have to quite thinking about Bethany other than she is going to be okay. I can't dwell on anything else." Leslie kept praying as she hurried toward the camp. She'd never prayed before but it relieved her mind to pray to Bethany's God for help. If she belonged to God, He would surely help her. It took almost fifteen minutes before she reach the camp.

"Eric, Bethany fell in a hole and I can't get her out. Please hurry. You need something for a ladder and some rope and something to lay her on to bring her up. She's unconscious. Hurry," Leslie exclaimed in a panic voice with tears running down her cheeks.

Albert was out of the plane and picked up some rope. If nothing else he'd carry her out of that hole.

"We need all the rope we can get. We might have to make a rope ladder. We also need some pillows to make a bed for her. Get them and let's go. Someone stay in camp and the rest of us will go help her. Peter, why don't you stay here?" Albert suggested. He was taken no chances as to what they would need to get her out of that hole. He was hurrying after Leslie urging her to go faster.

"I'll stay here but please take a flare and let it go when everything is alright. I'll be worrying about her," Peter admitted.

The four men ran through the bushes. They could tell where the ladies had gone. Leslie had started to lead them but they soon ran past her. She followed close behind them. She tried to keep the tears from coming but they dropped down her cheeks anyway. She didn't know what they would find when they got back to that awful hole. "Please, God, let her be alive," she prayed again.

Albert was leading the group. A sick feeling came over him that Bethany could be hurt, crippled, or... He wouldn't finish the thought. She was going to be all right. She had to be. She was the camp cook and they needed her, but not just for cooking. He needed her as she was his friend. No matter what he did, Bethany still was his friend. He had to hope that she would be all right.

The thoughts just made him hurry all the more and some of the rest of the group were having a hard time keeping up with him. Soon he was at the spot that Leslie had described to them. It was a clear area just like she told them. It looked as though it might have been farm land at one time.

"The hole is to your right, Albert," yelled Leslie.

Albert walked to his right a ways and then spotted the hole. "Bethany, speak to me," he pleaded.

No response came from the unconscious girl in the hole.

He looked at her as the other men gathered around the hole. "She's definitely unconscious. We have to get her out of there right now. I'm going to be the one that goes down into the hole after her," Albert declared.

"Albert," Eric said gently. "Are you a medic? Do you know what to do if she has a broken neck? Do you know how to try to revive her? She needs someone who has a little medical training."

Albert ducked his head. Once again Eric was right. He hated the thoughts of the man touching Bethany but he knew that was the best way to help her. "You're right," he exclaimed and said no more about it.

Jim and Dennis tied the rope to a tree and Eric let himself down into the hole with one of the ropes. He knew he couldn't bring Bethany back up that way. The men were already working on a type of bed so they could lay Bethany on it and perhaps tie her on it and then lift her out of the hole using the rope bed. Albert was almost in the way more than helping. He was so upset over Bethany that he wasn't thinking straight at least in Eric's opinion.

Eric was pleased that he thought to get his first aid kit at the last minute before they left. He had a feeling he was going to need it. The airplane had a good kit and there should be medical equipment in there that would help with Bethany's condition. He could make sure her blood pressure was all right and that she was getting enough oxygen in her lungs.

When he reached the area where she was, he knelt beside her and prayed first. Then he felt her pulse. Yes, there was a pulse and it was pretty strong. That was good. Then he looked her over. There was a big bump on the head but it didn't appear that the neck was broken. That was his main worry. Never the less he would put a neck brace on her since that was what he was taught.

"What's going on down there," Albert yelled.

"Albert, she has a good pulse. I've put a neck brace on her just as a precaution," Eric told him.

Then Eric carefully opened one of her eyes. This was not good. They looked as though she had a concussion. It was a matter of how bad the concussion was. This could go on for some days. He knew cases where the patients were unconscious for two weeks. He sure hoped this wasn't the way it would be with Bethany. But he thought he'd shake her shoulders a little and call her name. He knew Albert was watching and if he didn't do that, he would wonder why.

"Bethany," Eric said and shook her gently.

It was just as he knew it would be. There was no response. Now they needed to get her out of the hole. "How is that bed or chair coming along? Have you been able to make some type of equipment to pull her out of this hole? I've checked her arms and legs and nothing is broken. She has a pretty good bump on her head. I believe she'll be unconscious for some time. So if you send down a chair type we'll need to tie her in. But a bed would be much better."

"The hole isn't big enough to bring the bed up," Albert exclaimed and immediately started clearing out the tree limbs and other things that blocked the way to the top. While he and Dennis cleared the way, Jim let down the makeshift bed.

"Is that going to work?" Jim asked. "Bringing those pillows was sure a good idea. That helped make a pretty good bed. Now what do you think, Eric, do you think you can put her on this contraption safely so we can bring her up. I've made four ropes for all four of us here to lift her out."

"It's going to work great. I'm glad you thought about lifting her out that way. That will be much better than if I tried to bring her up. Now I'm going to carefully put her on the rope bed."

Eric slowly moved Bethany's head and shoulders onto the bed. She never groaned or made a move. He didn't like that. She needed to at least moan in pain. But he said nothing to the audience that was watching him. He didn't want to discourage anyone. He knew that Leslie was just about to go ballistic. The two girls had formed a good friendship over the weeks that they had been there on the island.

Finally, he was able to get the rest of her body on the rope bed. The men and Leslie each had a rope waiting for Eric to give them the signal to pull it up.

"Now, go very slow in bringing the bed up. Don't get in a hurry and everyone try to pull together. I think she's in the bed securely, but if one pulls too hard and it goes sideways, she could always fall out. Just be careful," Eric instructed. He knew he probably didn't have to say that, but he did anyway. He was nervous about this whole thing. If Bethany would just moan, move, sigh or do anything, he would feel better. But she lay as one of the... He wouldn't even think that. He couldn't.

Everyone was pulling slowly. It took a while for them to learn to pull evenly so the bed wouldn't tip over. When they finally were successful in bringing the bed to the top of the hole, Jim said for them all to go to the right, his right and slowly let the bed down on firm ground. It worked perfectly.

Albert quickly knelt down by her side. He took her hand. "Bethany, Bethany, can you hear me?" he asked.

Nothing. No response at all from the girl.

Eric climbed up the rope. "Now I suggest that you men start cutting a path to the camp. Use the path we came on and make it wide enough for the rope bed to go through the path. Jim and Dennis, you two do that and Leslie can help you. Albert and I will carry Bethany on the bed. We'll take this slowly so that we don't drop her or have some branches or vines scratch her. We need to get her back in good condition."

"Did you try to wake her up," asked Albert impatiently. A little restorative would bring her right around.

"I shook her gently and called her name but that's all," Eric admitted.

"Why didn't you try a restorative? That would wake her right up. Here let me give her one," Albert insisted.

"Albert," Eric said calmly although he didn't feel that way. He'd like to knock him in the head to get his attention but he answered him carefully. "At this point, it wouldn't be wise to give her a restorative. I looked at her eyes. They are too glassy. We need to wait for a while, maybe even a couple of days before we try that. Just try to be patient. Let's get her back to camp and in her bed first."

Albert said nothing. He just hoped that Eric knew what he was talking about. He just didn't like him from the first day. He reminded him of his father. Always right about everything and never wrong. But he had to admit that medicine was one thing he knew nothing about.

So he'd say nothing and let Medic Eric help Bethany if he could. He wondered if she was in pain, but she wasn't groaning so he assumed that she wasn't.

Several times the group had to stop and rest. It wasn't easy making a path wide enough for Bethany's bed to be carried through it. It wasn't easy carrying the bed with the weight on it through the brush and vines they had to walk over.

"Let's take another rest," Eric announced. It will do us no good to be totally exhausted when we get her back to camp. Right now she's sleeping peacefully and that's good."

"We just rested a little bit ago," Albert complained. He just wanted to get the girl back to camp and in a good bed. He still wasn't sure that she was going to make it. That bulge on her head was not a good thing.

"Bethany is doing all right, Albert. She's in no danger. You men made a good rope bed for her. The pillows make it soft. There's so sense in killing ourselves in the process of bringing her to camp."

Albert said nothing more. Once again Mr. Know It All seemed to have the last word. Well, there was nothing he could do but go along with it. He just wished that Bethany would respond to him or even moan or groan. But she just lay there. He had to admit that her color looked all right. She hadn't lost any blood and Eric said her pulse was good. He just couldn't stop thinking about her.

Eric kept watching Bethany for any sign of movement. There was none. He knew that was not uncommon but not being a doctor, he'd feel a lot better if she'd move around. They were almost to the camp. It would be a relief when they reached their destination.

He looked at Leslie. Every now and then a tear fell. He wished there was some way he could reassure her.

He heard Jim talking to her. "She has a strong pulse, Leslie. That means she's going to be fine. Now don't you worry any more about Bethany."

Leslie smiled. It was hard not to worry but she'd try. She kept watching Bethany as they carried her on the bed. That bump was too big to suit Leslie. That was why she was unconscious. Her head must have hit a rock or something down there. She should have stayed with

Bethany and not parted, but then both of them might have been in the hole and that wouldn't have been good.

They were almost to camp. Everyone was going to be so, tired. How was she going to have enough energy to try to cook some dinner for the men when she was so tired? She didn't even know that much about cooking except for what she watched Bethany do. Perhaps one of the men would help her make dinner or they could just eat some of those energy bars and have a can of juice.

CHAPTER 12

Caring for the Invalid

When they finally reached the camp, everyone was pleased but very tired. It had taken longer than they thought it would to clear the way and carry the rope bed through the path and into the camp. By the time they got there, they were tired and very hungry.

"Hey, I smell something cooking. Boy does it smell good," Dennis exclaimed. He sniffed the air a couple of times.

They all liked the smell of whatever it was that was cooking. Good old Peter, he had cooked their lunch. It was venison steaks and it looked as though he had some type of salad. Was that mashed potatoes he had there? What ever it was, Eric knew that all of them would appreciate the meal. They had all worked hard getting Bethany back to camp. They were tired but not too tired to eat.

"How is she?" Peter asked.

"She's unconscious and will be for a while. If it's too long, I think there is a feeding tube in this medical kit. But I'm hoping not to use it. We'll give her a day or two before we do that. I've checked her eyes from time to time and I do believe they are clearing up a little. That's a real good sign," Eric remarked.

Peter came over and looked at her. Yes she was unconscious and would be for a while. He'd seen this type of accident before and he could tell by looking at the girl that she was hurt. He could even see the bump on her head. It was in a bad place for a bump. He looked at Eric and knew that he had figured that out but evidently he hadn't told any of the rest of them. So Peter said nothing.

After they had placed Bethany into her bed making sure that she was comfortable, they all went out and enjoyed their lunch as much as they could under the circumstances. Every one of them loved Bethany. She always had something nice to say and treated everyone special. They each wondered how long it would take before she awoke. So therefore the meal was mostly eaten in silence.

Jim finally spoke up. "The last thing that Bethany would have wanted for us to be is gloomy and sad. We need to go on about our work and not let this get us down. So far we have had a fairly good time surviving. Now in a day or two, she'll likely wake up and she won't want to think that all we did was to sit around and moan, groan and worry about her."

"Jim's right. Let's finish the lunch and get back to work," Eric suggested.

"I think that we should go back there and search that place thoroughly. Why was that hole there? What was beyond there? There's no telling what we might find that would be useful if we went looking," Dennis remarked.

"Good idea," Eric agreed. "Why don't you and Jim go back there only be really careful about the holes? Where there is one, there could be more. It sure seems that someone lived there at one time which gives us some hope that we could find things we need and that sometime someone would come back to the island."

Both men took another look at the sleeping Bethany and then headed back to see what they could find. They hoped to find some type of evidence that life existed there at one time. The area where Bethany and Leslie went looked as though it had been farmed at one time. And that hole Bethany fell in sure looked like a trap for animals or perhaps enemies.

Peter and Albert worked on the plane. The engine was just about ready to start working properly. It gave them a lot more enthusiasm to hurry and get it running right. They knew that another month would bring colder weather and they needed to be prepared. So far it had been rather nice since they landed on the island. They could make the airplane a lot warmer than their shelter if they had to spend the winter there. But they sure hoped they didn't have to.

Peter and Albert knew that they could get the engine running but they wondered if the others thought they were working to obtain the impossible. It probably looked that way to them. None of them seemed to be too enthusiastic about it. "They're going to be one shocked group of people when we start that engine running," Albert thought. He could almost picture their faces.

Leslie began to think about what to prepare for their dinner. She wasn't much of a cook but she would try. She had watched Bethany cook, but she had no idea which of those herbs to use in which dish. But then, Peter's lunch had tasted so good. He must know a little about cooking. She would go and ask him.

She walked over to the plane and spotted Peter on the outside. "Peter, you sure cooked a good lunch. I'm not a very good cook. I'm not like Bethany. I've never had to cook. I watched her but she did most of the work. I just did what she asked me to. Can you help me with the seasoning? I thought I'd try for a stew. I can put everything in it and get it cooking if you would season it for me."

Peter smiled at her. "If you won't tell anyone, I'll tell you a secret. I used to be a chef in a restaurant. But keep that secret. Bethany does a great job cooking and she loves it so we'll let her have the job when she wakes up."

"I heard that," Albert said. "Chef Peter, sound good to me. Bethany will be glad to have a rest from cooking now and then."

"I'm threatening you, Albert, if you tell anyone about this you'll be in big trouble. I don't want to do the cooking. I just knew you would all be exhausted when you came back from helping Bethany so I cooked lunch. One word, my friend and …" Peter didn't finish.

Albert laughed.

That was the first time Leslie had heard Albert laugh. He seemed to have changed quite a bit since the airplane crashed. He sure was more agreeable. It was good to hear the man laugh.

"I'm going to walk a ways to find some roots to put in the stew. We found some wild onions the other day and we could use those to give it a little flavor." Leslie started to walk away.

"Wait, Leslie, under the circumstances, I don't think you should go alone. I'll go with you. What I'm doing will keep. I don't think any of us should go for a walk alone anymore. If Bethany had been alone, we'd never have found her. I think we should establish a rule that at least two people go when they leave camp," Eric remarked with conviction.

"That's a good idea," Peter agreed. "We sure don't want anymore accidents. We need to watch out for brush that's piled up as it was over that hole. We all need to be very careful."

While Eric didn't know all that much about gathering roots, edible grasses, or berries, he did enjoy the time spent with Leslie. When they came to the berry patch, he picked berries. When there were roots to dig, he dug them but he let Leslie pick the greens. He wasn't too sure about them.

"Look, Eric, there are mushrooms here. Oh, boy, that'll add flavor to anything we cook," Leslie exclaimed excitedly.

"But Leslie, aren't there a lot of poison mushrooms? Do you know the difference between the good ones and the poison ones? I don't think I want to eat any of them. I've read too many articles about poison mushrooms," he remarked definitely.

"Eric, I was raised gathering mushrooms in the fields. Look, this is a good one but that one there is a poison one. I definitely know the difference. I'd suggest you let me gather the mushrooms. You pick some more berries or dig some more roots." Leslie laughed. She had an idea some of her island friends would holler when she brought the mushrooms into camp. She'd have to eat them first to show the rest of them that she knew the difference between the good ones and the poison ones.

The two soon had their packs full and headed back to camp.

"This has been a nice change of pace from what I usually do, Leslie. I've enjoyed gathering the food supplies. I just may come again. You ladies sure found a good area. We won't starve as long as we can dig, gather greens, and pick berries. I could add find mushrooms but I'm not too sure about that."

Leslie laughed.

"Go ahead and laugh. After you survive the mushrooms, I just may try one." Eric laughed with her. He was quite sure she knew what she was doing but then there were those tales out there about poison mushrooms.

"Have you seen our winter supply, Eric? We've a lot of extra food dried so just in case we have to spend the winter, we'll still have food to eat. We always put away several days supply for winter every time we come and gather the food," Leslie informed him.

"I had no idea that you had so much saved. That's great. We hope to get out of here before then, but each day we're here the chances look slimmer. The only hope we have is to get the airplane engine going and plug in some cell phones. Then we'll need to walk up the mountain and try to reach someone." Eric hadn't lost all hope of getting off the island. He still believed they'd be able to reach someone with their cell phones once they had them charged up.

He knew that a lot of different things could happen that would let them return home, but with no airplanes going overhead and no ships sailing by the island, how would they be found? He just prayed that somehow someone would come by. Some ship or plane could come by and see their signals. And he hadn't ruled out God. He was the God of miracles and right now they needed to hope for one.

About the time they reached camp, Dennis and Jim came back from their exploration of the area where Bethany had fallen into the hole. They had gone a little further than they had before and found some interesting things and among them some skeletons. When they returned to camp, the group asked if they had found anything interesting.

"Only some skeletons," Dennis said. "Now what are we going to have to eat this evening. What are you cooking, Peter?"

"Just frying up some mushrooms," he replied nonchalantly.

Dennis eyes widened. "Don't bother to fry some for me. I know there are poison ones out there and if anyone got a poison mushroom it would be me." No, sir, he wasn't going to eat any of them.

Leslie watched the group when she and Peter prepared the mushrooms. Dennis wasn't the only one with a shocked look on his face. Peter knew that the mushrooms were good but he was amused that the others wouldn't trust his judgment.

"I'll tell you what, I'll eat the first bite and if I don't fall down dead, one of you can have the second bite," Peter suggested.

"I'll wait until morning and see if you're still with us," declared Albert.

"I'm with Albert," Dennis exclaimed.

"Peter, you worked in a restaurant. You saw lots of mushrooms in the different food, isn't that right?" Eric asked.

"I sure did. I know good ones from bad ones. It's easy to tell once you learn the difference. I'm not going to put them in the food. I'll just fry them up for now and anyone who trusts Leslie and I can eat some with us. If you don't trust our judgment, don't eat them but you're going to miss a great dish."

Peter was rather amused. He was a cook and Leslie had lived in the wilderness and often took trips where their group only ate what was in the place where they were going. And yet, Albert and Dennis didn't trust them. Jim hadn't said a word. He was watching the whole thing with a slight smile. Jim was the quiet one in the bunch. Dennis always had something to say.

Peter kept cooking the mushrooms while Leslie prepared the rest of the food. Eric watched Peter and Leslie as they cooked. That was usually Bethany's job but it was nice to know that there were others who could do a pretty good job of cooking. Even when Bethany became conscience, she wouldn't be able to cook for a while. She'd have to have some time to recuperate from the fall.

Eric decided that he would eat the mushrooms because he trusted Leslie. They smelled good while they were cooking. It was amazing how many different things they found on this island to eat.

"Did you ever think that our skeletons might have eaten mushrooms and that was what did them in?" Dennis remarked.

Eric burst out laughing along with Peter and Leslie. "Didn't you say that they were sitting up as if they were talking? If the mushrooms had killed them, each one would have been holding his stomach in pain and lying on the ground."

Finally everything was cooked and the group sat down at the table. Leslie, Eric and Peter all took a good helping of mushrooms along with the other food.

Albert walked over to Peter. "Are you sure they're all right?" he asked seriously. He had become pretty good friends with Peter. He sure wouldn't want something to happen to him. And he had heard all sorts of things about bad mushrooms. One mushroom looked the same to him as another one.

"I've cooked lots of mushrooms and these are very familiar. I know they're good and so does Leslie. Albert you should have some with us. They're really the good kind of mushroom. Poison mushrooms look very different," he assured the doubting man.

"If you say so, I'll eat some," Albert said reluctantly. But Leslie noticed he only put two small slices on his plate. She watched now and then to see if he'd actually eat them. Finally he took a slice out of one and put it in his mouth. Immediately, he seemed to know that it was all right and he ate the other mushroom on his plate.

Peter laughed. "I wanted so much to hold my stomach and roll on the ground after eating that mushroom, but I couldn't make myself. As frightened as you two seemed to be, I decided that it might give someone a heart attack. But it would have been funny. But I don't think now was an appropriate time for a joke."

"It sure isn't," Albert agreed.

"If you had done that, I'd have had a heart attack, believe me," Jim remarked. "I'm so hungry for some mushrooms but I'm just a little leery about eating them. But it appears you're all doing okay so far. I think I'll wait until morning, though before I try any. Someone has to survive to take care of the camp."

"You and I will be the only survivors, Jim. But we can handle things. We sure will have lots of extra food to eat. I sure hope you can cook because I can't," Dennis admitted to his friend.

"I can't cook either. Perhaps we better pray that at least Peter or Leslie survives these mushrooms so we have a cook."

"That's not a bad idea," Jim remarked and grinned.

Dennis and Jim didn't have any mushrooms. Jim figured they were probably all right but he decided not to have any. If no one was sick tomorrow from them, then he just might try one. He had to be careful of what he ate. He was pretty sure he wasn't allergic to mushrooms. But he did have some bad allergies. It's a wonder they hadn't kicked up with all the strange food he had eaten on this island.

On the other hand, it's a good thing his allergies hadn't kicked up as there was no doctor to go to for a shot.

CHAPTER 13

Some Good News

Peter helped Leslie do the cooking while Bethany was ill. They prepared a good lunch and then decided that they'd make the mushroom soup for dinner. They'd worried about a cook since Bethany had her accident and even if she became conscious, she wouldn't be able to work for two or three days.

Eric was pleased that there was another cook in camp. He and the rest of the men watched Peter as he helped Leslie prepare the meals. He sure seemed to know what he was doing. Fancy was what the food items looked like when he finished preparing them. Eric grinned. Although it was nice to have it look attractive, all they needed was something to eat.

"Well, Chef Peter, just where did you get your degree in cooking?" Jim asked sarcastically with a grin.

"He was once a chef in a restaurant," Albert remarked and laughed. "He doesn't want anyone to know that so don't tell anyone."

Albert kept laughing along with all of the others except for Peter. He glared at Albert with a glare that said, "I'm going to get even with you."

They ate the quick lunch and then went back to work. There always seemed to be something to do. One job was finished and then there was something else to do. Eric was pleased as he knew it was much better to keep his crew busy than for them to sit around and pity themselves for being stuck on an island. That sure wouldn't do them any good.

It was a tried looking crew that sat down to eat their dinner. Eric looked around. Everyone was enjoying the delicious stew. So Peter was a cook as well as a news reporter—a man of many talents. The noon meal had been very simple so they didn't have a chance to really taste Peter's cooking until the evening when they had the stew. They took a vote and declared it excellent.

The group was sitting around the fire as they usually do. Jim played his harmonica as he did almost every night since everyone insisted on it. Sometimes they sang along and other times they just listened to what he played. How so much music could come out of the little instrument was a mystery to all of them. And Jim did a great job playing that harmonica. They hadn't heard anyone that could do any better.

Eric could tell that Albert wanted to question him some more. "Albert, tomorrow we'll try to wake Bethany. Sometime in the afternoon would be the best time. We need a full twenty-four hours or more to pass before we force her to wake up. Even then, I need to look at her eyes and make sure they are clearing up some more."

"But she hasn't eaten all day," objected Albert.

"She had breakfast yesterday. She's fine. She can go 48 hours easily without water or food but I'm hoping we don't have to wait that long. I looked at her earlier and she's looking better. I'm sure that she's going to be all right."

Albert only nodded. Quack doctors didn't impress him much but that was all that was available.

"Jim and Dennis, what did you find on your excursion besides those skeletons?" Eric asked.

Dead silence. Both of the men looked upset when he asked the question. It was plain that they didn't want to talk about what they found.

"I think that you should tell us, friends. We need to know. Evidently it was something that upset you. Now, what could you have found that was so terrible you didn't want to tell the rest of us?" Eric asked.

"Eric, we found skeletons all right. There is no telling how long they've been there. But it wasn't too reassuring. However, we don't know what happened and how they happen to be there. With an imagination like mine, all kinds of things could have happened to the people who belonged to the skeletons. But it did rather throw cold water on our hopes of getting out of here," Jim remarked rather sadly. He couldn't get over the way the skeletons were.

"You should have seen them. They were sitting up under a tree. Just as if they were sitting there having a cup of coffee and a conversation with each other," Dennis remarked. "It was weird, let me tell you. It gave me the heebie geebies. But old Jim here, I think he was ready to shake hands with them. He's one cold dude. I wanted to get out of there as soon as we saw them but he wanted to examine them a little closer. Ugh is all I can say. I'm not too eager to see a scene like that again. That place is spooky, let me tell you. You could almost feel that those skeletons were going to talk to you any minute. They were going to tell us to get out of their area!"

Everyone had to laugh even if it wasn't a laughing matter. The way Dennis told it was a little too humorous to keep from laughing.

"There were more things there than just the skeletons. There was evidence that people had been living there. I know that Dennis thought he was walking through a graveyard. But it was interesting and a little spooky as well. It was as if we were invading their territory and we shouldn't be there. Now I know that that's a bunch of nonsense but that was the feeling that it gave us," Jim explained.

"Perhaps I'll walk over there with someone tomorrow and look around a little more. If there were people living here at one time, they had to have some type of shelter. I could look a little closer at the skeletons to see if I could figure out how they died. I don't think they would have died of malnutrition. There's too much to eat on this island. But it's worth checking out," Eric stated.

"I volunteer Jim to go with you. I'll stay here and help Leslie with the gathering of the food. That idea of having two people go together when they walk is a good one. There's no telling what could happen," Dennis stated.

"Sure, volunteer me, old buddy. Remember, I don't get mad, I just get even," Jim threatened.

They all decided that it was just about time they headed for bed. It made for a nice time to sit around the fire and talk. Eric found out that none of the survivors had ever been married. That seemed strange. You would have thought that out of seven survivors, one or two would have a spouse. He was twenty-eight and he would guess that Dennis and Jim were close to his age. But he was sure that Albert was in his thirties. Peter was a little younger, if he guessed right but then you couldn't always tell someone's age. Some people looked a lot younger than they actually were.

After a good night's sleep, the team woke up fairly early the next morning. Again Peter helped Leslie make breakfast. He had ground the roots and the mushrooms and with some eggs had made some pancakes which they could put some berries on. Peter watched as they ate the slightly unusual pancakes.

"These are good. I'll bet there are more vitamins in these pancakes than any I ever ate before," declared Dennis. "Since you all survived the fried mushrooms and the mushroom soup, I'll eat some now. Just wasn't going to take any chances."

"They sure are good," Eric exclaimed and Jim and Albert agreed. By now just about anything tasted good. It had been so long since they had anything really sweet so they didn't miss the honey or syrup on the pancakes. And that's a good thing, thought Eric. They didn't need to dwell on what they could eat back home. He was rather proud of the group because they weren't focusing on what they would be doing back home. They weren't there so there wasn't any sense in making themselves feel regret because they didn't have everything they had at home.

Peter and Albert went to work with a smile. They had a secret but they weren't going to tell anyone just yet. It wouldn't be long before they would all know their secret. They tried not to smile or look too suspicious but Albert was having a hard time keeping quiet. He could hardly wait.

"Please don't go too far away from camp for the next few minutes," Peter suggested. "We may need your help." That was all he said as he and Albert walked to the airplane. Peter sat in the pilots chair and Albert stayed outside by the engine watching it.

In only moments they heard a roar—a loud roar. Everyone was startled except the two airplane mechanics. Albert watched as their eyes stared at the airplane. It was just as he thought; they didn't think it was possible for anyone to repair one of the engines.

Soon they saw the plane slowly leave the water and creep upon the shore. Everyone was clapping and dancing around. They shook their heads. Peter and Albert had been working on that engine for weeks and now it was up and running. It shocked them all. They'd been busy with their jobs and had left Peter and Albert to repair the airplane engine but had almost given up expecting any positive results.

"Where do you want me to park this thing, Eric?" asked Peter yelling as loud as he could over the roar of the engine.

Eric motioned his hands to where he thought would be a good place to park the airplane and Peter drove it right upon the beach where Eric wanted it.

Peter and Albert were all smiles. "What do you think of our little surprise we had for you this morning," asked Peter.

"Little surprise, I'd say it was a big surprise," Dennis quipped.

Eric just shook his head. "Get a couple of cell phones while the engine is running and plug them in." Jim hurried into the plane and plugged three of them into the electrical outlets. They would have to let the engine run for a while to get the batteries charged. The group began to think that there would be a possibility now to reach someone if they went up the mountain and made the call from one of the cell phones.

Everyone was so excited. Eric liked the idea of having something to encourage the crew instead of something like what Jim and Dennis found. Now there certainly was a little better chance that they could reach someone.

They each had to pat Albert and Peter on the back and tell them they thought they were the best mechanics ever. Both men didn't mind that at all. They had a tough task to do and it took a long time but they were successful. They felt a little praise didn't hurt them any.

"Albert and Peter, you two are the greatest. I had my doubts with all the damage done to the engines that any of them could ever be fixed but you two didn't give up. We all want to thank you. This is a good thing. Thanks to both of you," Eric exclaimed.

"When we get back home and I have any car trouble at all, I know where I'm going to bring my automobile, I'll take it right to the Albert and Peter's Garage," Dennis remarked smiling.

"Yeah, you do that," Albert sneered. "You're going to have to find it first."

While all this was going on, no one noticed someone coming out of the shelter and staring at the plane.

"What's all this noise going on? How can anyone sleep with that roaring engine?" Bethany asked the group.

"Bethany," Leslie said with tears in her eyes. "Bethany, you're all right. Let's back away from the engine a little so we can talk. Do you feel all right?"

"Other than a bad headache which that roaring engine doesn't help, I feel okay. What happened? I remember falling in a hole and that's all. I don't remember coming back to camp. What's going on? Oh, wait a minute, that's the airplane making that noise. So they really did get the engine working," Bethany remarked. She wasn't thinking too clearly because the airplane was no longer in the water but up on the shore. She felt a little hazy about everything.

"You had a concussion, according to Dr. Eric. The men made a rope bed and got you out of the hole and brought you back to camp. We have been so worried about you. It's so good to see you awake," Leslie declared.

Albert came over and smiled at her. "Bethany, I'm so glad that you're okay. I worried about you. It is so nice to see you walking around. But you have to take it easy. No cooking for a couple of days. We have a chef in the camp and he and Leslie can do the cooking."

"Thanks, Albert. Thanks to everyone for helping me out of that hole. I just wish I had an aspirin for this headache," Bethany exclaimed holding her head with her hands. The roar didn't do anything to help the pain.

"Dr. Eric to your service," Eric exclaimed. "Bethany, it's only natural that you have a headache after the concussion. Now, I have some aspirins in the medical kit from the airplane. It's right in the shelter on the shelf. Let me get them for you." Eric hurried and retrieved the aspirin along with a glass of water.

"What Albert said about you not cooking is right. You need rest. You can walk around and watch, but you shouldn't do anything strenuous. Just pull up a chair, that is a log, and sit down and relax. You can even give orders and we'll obey them," Eric promised and smiled at the weak young lady.

"But I should help do something. I'll just do things that don't take any effort, how would that be? I promise not to exert myself. I have to admit that I feel a little weak after my fall. But if I had a concussion, I guess I would feel weak-kneed." Bethany walked over to where the group was. She hoped the aspirins kicked in pretty soon. She could never remember having such a bad headache before.

"Okay, but no gathering food or walking in the woods for two or three days. I'll see how you are by then and decide if you can go back to work. Now tell me honestly, you feel a little shaky don't you?" Eric asked.

Bethany didn't particularly like the idea of doing nothing, but she knew that Eric was probably right. "Yes, I do feel weak and shaky and I'm hungry. Is there one of those energy bars around here? I feel like I haven't eaten in two days. How about an herbal tea to go along with my health bars?"

"Coming right up," Albert said and went to the food supply and brought her two bars and poured the hot water over the herbs. It was good they kept the fire going and a pan of water on it at all times.

"Well, this has been a good day," Eric exclaimed. "The airplane engine is working and our Miss Bethany is awake. We need to celebrate. What are you two cooks going to cook tonight to celebrate these two happenings?"

"How about we have a berry pie?" Peter asked. He knew that he could take the ground roots and make into flour and a little fat that was saved from the deer or rabbit and make pastry. He set right out to do that. He agreed with Eric. This called for a celebration.

"Peter, I'm going to shut the engine off now and give us a little peace and quiet. It's been on long enough to charge the batteries." Albert walked into the airplane and turned the engine off. He checked his cell phone and it was charged.

It was nice and quiet once the engine was shut down! They had all moved a distance away from the noisy engine and were glad when the noise ceased. It did sound rather nice at first though. They knew that by bringing the airplane out of the water, they could retrieve more things out of the storage area. When the airplane was driven upon the beach, a lot of water poured out of the luggage compartment.

Eric had watched as the water drained through the hole they had made. But he knew that they needed a hole in the bottom of the luggage department. So he took the sharp rocks and started in. It didn't take long before all the water came flowing out. It would take a while before the luggage compartment was dry but it was going to be a good place to store things if they had to spend the winter on the island.

It was very difficult to get into the airplane. They needed more than that make shift ladder. What could they do to make getting into the airplane a lot easier? He couldn't think right now. Eric decided to ask the resident engineer.

"Albert," Eric said slowly. "It's going to be hard getting in and out of that airplane with that makeshift ladder. Do you think you could design an easier entrance to the airplane entrance? There are a lot of the poles around here. Now that we have tools to work with, perhaps you could design some actual steps into the airplane. What do you think?"

"I'll get right at it. How wide do you want the steps? Someone get that axe and saw that we found and bring some poles. We're about to make steps into our new home," Albert exclaimed.

The poles were gathered and the equipment Albert needed was given to him. He ordered the poles cut four feet in length. He said they would need at least 20 poles for the steps. He would need some poles about seven feet to reach the plane. Eric watched as the group prepared the steps according to what Albert told them.

When they were all ready, they carefully tied the steps together with the rope they had found in the luggage department. When it was all over, the steps were pretty impressive. Eric sure liked the idea of rope holding the steps together rather than vines. You never knew whether the vines would begin to dry up and become fragile. Each time he walked into the airplane he had double checked the vines.

"Who's going to be the first one to use the steps?" Albert asked.

"I am," Bethany remarked. She promptly walked up the steps and into the airplane. "They work great, Albert," she declared and smiled down at all of them.

It was a good job, Eric thought. Everyone helped and they had it done in no time at all.

Eric knew that they could get to the luggage compartment through the airplane or they could climb in through the hole they made. He

CHAPTER 14

A Strange Radio

Eric wasn't going to wait for the luggage compartment to dry. He took one of the flashlights and headed into the compartment. He was followed by Jim and Dennis. They were all curious as to what they would find.

"Peter, would you and Albert get the luggage and other things we find? We'll hand them out to you," Eric suggested.

"Sure will," Peter agreed.

"I can help," Leslie exclaimed.

"Leslie, why don't you go through the suitcases as Peter and Albert give them to you?" Eric requested.

"Will do," she answered.

"I'm just supposed to sit here and do nothing?" Bethany asked. She was a little tired of doing nothing.

"You can help Leslie, but don't exert yourself," ordered Albert and grinned at the invalid.

"Thanks," she answered and returned his smile. She knew that Albert was very concerned about her. She appreciated him wanting to take care of her and not let her over-do but at the same time, she was bored doing nothing.

Eric was surprised at how much more there was in the compartment. He also found some more tools which they could use. He figured that they probably were there for situations just like they were in now. If they could have had these tools when they first landed that would have helped lots but the crash caused a hole in the side of the luggage compartment and then it took on water.

With everyone helping, Eric decided it wasn't going to take too long to empty the compartment. The relay system was working very well. He was handing the items to Dennis and Dennis handed them to Jim and Jim handed them to Peter or Albert and they took them over to the two ladies.

When they were all through, they looked at the huge stack of luggage and other items. Many of the things they found they could make good use of. Eric watched as everyone worked. Once again he thought about what a good group of people they were. If he'd had a bunch of people that wouldn't cooperate they'd never have accomplished all that they had done so far.

"Hey, Eric, take a look at this," Leslie exclaimed as she held up a radio. "It looks like more than a normal radio. It's one you can broadcast with. It was in an airtight suitcase so it didn't get wet. Who knows how to operate this? I know a little about it but not a whole lot."

"Wow," Albert all but yelled. "Let me have a look at that. Leslie, let's put our heads together and see if we can get it working."

When they turned it on, they heard music. Then they turned the dial and heard some news. Everyone wanted to hear the news. They heard some preliminary news and then they heard something very interesting to all of them.

The news wasn't a lot different than usual but it was just nice to hear the what was going on in the world. They heard them say that flight 509 hadn't closed their flight and nothing was heard from them. If any of them survived and happened to be listening to the news, it would be good to try the radio.

"We took that radio out but we haven't done anything with it. Let's start working on it again," Eric suggested.

"While you're working on that, I'm going to study this foreign radio. I'll bet there is a way to send messages if we just knew how'" Albert declared.

Eric and Peter worked on the radio some and put it back in the airplane. "If we can get it to work just enough to say flight 509, I'll bet someone would pass the word on to our tower," Peter stated.

"You're right. Tomorrow we'll start the airplane again and we'll see what happens," Eric answered.

"Say, how is the broadcasting on the radio working. Are you getting anywhere? Can you reach anyone?" Dennis asked.

"Leslie and I haven't quite figured this thing out. It is far different than any radio configuration that I've used in the past. But give us time and we shall figure it out. Isn't that right, Leslie?"

"I'm sure we can. We're close, but like Albert said, it's different. It appears to be a foreign radio. But we won't give up. Sooner or later we'll figure it out," promised Leslie. She always liked a puzzle. It intrigued her. She wouldn't quit working on it even if Albert did. She had an idea he had the same thoughts she had.

Eric came over and looked over their shoulder. He had to agree that it was built a little different than anything he had ever seen. But he had only worked with short wave radios that didn't transmit very far. This looked as though it would transmit a lot further if they discovered how to use it. It was a big outfit.

"Just what piece of luggage did you take the radio out of?" Eric asked.

Leslie walked over to the particular suitcase and showed Eric. He had some ideas he wanted to check out. He looked at the clothing. Yes that confirmed his suspicions. He glanced at a book that was found in the luggage. It was written in a foreign language. The language appeared to be similar to Spanish but he wasn't quite sure. It was definitely a radio used by a foreigner.

Eric looked all through the luggage and nothing else seemed to be of interest. He didn't remember burying any foreigners, but then there were many white people who lived overseas. They weren't all in America.

The group worked hard all day going through the luggage. Some of the things inside were soaking wet. Other suitcases were airtight and they carefully looked through these. They found some food, but not a lot. But anything different was always a treat. Eric knew that the group would appreciate anything different now and then. Most of the food items found in the luggage were desert items such as candy bars. It seemed that some people had a sweet tooth and didn't want to get in a place where they didn't have any desert.

When Dennis pulled out a lot of candy bars from one of the larger suitcases, everyone ran to take one. Candy sounded good to all of them. He did suggest that they each only eat one and save some for the next few days. Whoever this person was, he had a good supply of candy bars—all kinds.

"I wonder what the purpose of all those candy bars could be. He had a supply and a half of sweet bars. Do you suppose they were for him or maybe he was taking them to some of the children over in Europe where there is so much starvation?" Jim asked.

"That's a possibility," Eric replied.

"Yes, I don't think people would actually bring that many candy bars for just themselves. One could always buy a candy bar in a store wherever one might go. He or she must have been bringing them to those children who have nothing," Leslie commented.

"I'm with Leslie. It isn't feasible that someone would have that much of a sweet tooth and not become diabetic. But it's a nice treat. There are some of my favorite candy bars in that pile," Bethany exclaimed.

"I don't know and I don't care who these candy bars belong to, all I know is that I'm going to enjoy them," Albert declared.

"I'm right with you, Albert, I'm going to enjoy them too," Dennis professed.

CHAPTER 15

A Great Find

The next morning right after breakfast, the group continued to work on the suitcases. If there was something they could use and it was wet, they hung it up to dry. They tried to leave the suitcases open so the insides would dry.

"Jim, I want to walk over to where you saw those skeletons. Are you willing to go with me?"

"Sure. The scene didn't bother me as much as it did Dennis. I'm used to things like that."

"You are? Are you a medic or something?" Eric asked.

"No, I'm not. Don't know anything about medicine and never wanted to. The idea of being around sick people wasn't my idea of an occupation. It hurt me terribly when my mother was so sick and could hardly breathe. She was one sweet woman and to see her die when I was only seventeen sure made me realize that the medical field wasn't what I wanted. There were a lot better choices out there for me. I always wondered about how the nurses handle so many sick patients dying after their acquaintance with them. It's hard to watch people die. No the medical field wasn't an occupation for me."

The two walked on the path that had been trampled down by the group when they brought Bethany back on the rope bed. When they finally reached their destinations, both men stared at the skeletons. It seemed strange the position they were sitting in, thought Eric. It was as though they were talking to one another. He felt a little like Dennis in that he was invading their space.

"Do you have any idea why a person would die and be sitting in this position, Jim? If they starved to death they would be laying on the ground too weak to sit up. If they were poisoned they would be holding their stomachs and again lying on the ground. There is something not natural about this setting," Eric stated.

"I've never seen any corpse like this. If I were guessing, I'd say that someone killed them and then placed them like this. Or if they didn't kill them, they just placed them this way out of respect which is probably what happened. They could have died of almost anything. I believe there is a tribe or people that believe people should be sitting up after they die. That would be my guess," Jim explained.

"Wow, you sure know a lot about skeletons. I just figured out what your occupation is. You're an undertaker or mortician, aren't you?"

Jim smiled. "You guessed it. Now you know why I didn't want to tell the others. People have weird ideas about undertakers and morticians. But it's just a job and one I rather like. I like to take the bodies and make them look nice for the people who are so sorrowful because they lost a loved one. When the appearance of their loved one looks pleasing and usually better looking than they actually were, it seems to comfort them. It's nice to hear them say something about how good their mother or father or loved one looked. They leave feeling much better."

"I'll bet you could tell us a lot of stories around the camp fire," Eric stated.

"Well, I'd have to be selective. Some you wouldn't want to hear. But, Eric, you make some real good friends. As a Christian, I can pray with them if they allow me to. It is quite a mission field. I've led several people to the Lord through this occupation. The ones whose mother or father were Christians and they were left alone without them are so upset that they ready listen to God's Word. I'm not a preacher but I can tell them how to find Christ as their Savior."

"I think you're right. But we didn't come here to stare at those two skeletons. Let's look around a little more. Perhaps we should walk a little further west and see what's there. The whole area is different from the rest of the island we have seen. I do believe that it has been farmed at one time," Eric stated.

"I wanted to look around a little more before but old Dennis was torn up so badly after seeing the skeletons, I couldn't talk him into anything except going back to the camp. It really shook him up. And I have to admit, it did feel like we were invading their privacy. The skeletons sitting up as if they were having a conversation with one another sure got to Dennis."

"If your theory is right, we should find the body of a third person around here that might have put the skeletons in that position. Unless, of course, he left the island right after he finished the ritual. Let's do some thorough searching. There's enough work back at camp to keep everyone busy most of the day and they won't miss us," Eric suggested.

"Is that what you try to do, Eric, keep every one busy?" Jim remarked with a twinkle in his eyes.

"Well, you know good and well if they didn't have something to do they'd be sitting around wishing they could go home and be bored to pieces. When they're busy, they seem pretty happy. I just have to keep dreaming up things that will keep them busy as well as help us survive if we have to live very long on this island," Eric replied.

"I'd say you were doing a pretty good job of dreaming up work. But all the work you had them do was necessary for our survival. Say, wouldn't it be nice if they had that radio working when we got back. I know that Albert has been a pain sometimes but he's one smart dude. He'll figure it out. I have an idea that he was one good engineer. He seems to be getting along a little better all the time. Bethany has quite the effect on him," Jim stated.

"You're right. Bethany is a peacemaker. She's rather quiet most of the time but she has sort of taken Albert on as a project. I'm afraid without Bethany, Albert might never have cooperated. Hey, would you look at is this?"

"Wow, that's something," Jim exclaimed. "We better take it back to camp."

"But how could we get it back to our campsite? We can't lift it and it's going to be awfully heavy to drag. We'll need some help with it. But it will be nice to have. Is there anything else around here?"

The two started walking every place. They never did come across another skeleton but they sure discovered lots of items that proved that some time in the past some people lived right in that area. There were dishes, all broken. There were signs that there was possibly a shelter right close to them. It had to be way in the past, thought Eric. All the items appeared to be very old.

"Well, we can bring Albert and Peter back with us, but I don't think we ought to ask Dennis. If we made a sled, four of us should be able to pull the sled with the wood stove on it. I know that we could be rescued in a day or two, but what if it's a lot longer? This wood stove would come in real handy," Jim suggested.

"No, we won't invite Dennis. Even if we did invite him he probably wouldn't come. I have to admit that the two skeletons are a strange site to see. Jim, look over there. That's a stove pipe for the stove. I think we should take it back. If we had to spend cold days here before we're rescued, we could put the stove into the airplane and cut a hole for the stove pipe. We'd sure keep warm."

"You're right. I have thought that we need to work on something to keep us warm in the winter. Even if they find us and I'm sure they will... Let me start again, when they find us, how are they going to get us off the island. There is no place to land an airplane. I have a suspicion that the water is not deep enough where we are for a ship to sail in it. That's why I think it's going to be a while before we get off the island."

"I agree with that," Eric replied.

The two men walked back to the camp. As they walked they both threw out ideas on how to move that heavy wood stove.

"I think we're going to have to ask Engineer Albert Desmond for his opinion once more. I have to admit the man can figure out all sorts of problems. So we might as well save our brain power and wait to talk with him," Jim suggested.

"It does please the man to be asked. And he has been very cooperative here lately. I have to admit we needed him in our group of people, even if I didn't think so at first. How he and Peter got that plane engine fixed so it would work is beyond me. Peter admitted to me that it was mainly

Albert's doing. He just did what Albert told him to do. Didn't Albert say he was good at bossing?" Eric laughed.

"Yes he did. I rather suspicion that it was Albert who figured out how to fix the airplane engine. But Peter is a great helper if he doesn't know much about what he's doing," Jim stated.

"I hate to admit it, but we sure wouldn't be in as good a shape as we are if it weren't for all of Albert's solutions to our problems."

"I agree with you," Jim said.

CHAPTER 16

Fishing for Salmon

When Jim and Eric arrived at the camp, they found that the group had pretty much finished searching the luggage. Bethany and Leslie were fixing lunch with some of the food that was retrieved from the luggage. "It's nice not to have to cook for every meal," Leslie commented.

"You need a good rest," Bethany exclaimed. "I had a good rest. I was lazy while all of you worked so hard. Now I'm just fine and ought to be able to do my part of the work. I never did like just lying around doing nothing."

"Peter, we need you and Albert to help us bring something back to camp. We found a wood stove. I think it would make things a lot easier for our cooks. How about it, can you lend a hand?" Eric asked.

"A wood stove? Now that's going to be hard to transport. Those things are heavy," Albert exclaimed.

"Do you have any idea how we could transport the stove to our camp. What would be the easiest way possible to bring it to our shelter, Albert? We are open to suggestions," Jim remarked.

"Well, we found that wagon in the luggage department and didn't pay much attention to it. It was just a little kid's wagon that someone wanted to take to a child for a present. I think we might be able to use that," Albert suggested.

"I had forgotten all about that. You're absolutely right, Albert. That should do the trick. But won't we have to have someone clear a path to pull it through the bushes?" asked Jim.

"Yes, but not too wide, only wide enough to pull the wagon with width of the stove added. The path we made to bring Bethany back just needs the branches and vines moved out of the way so the wagon will pull a lot easier. We have trampled a lot of it down by walking to and from. We can take the axe we found and cut away at the vines and toss the branches out of the way. I think we should go bring it back right now," Albert suggested.

"Good idea, Albert," Eric remarked. He had forgotten completely about the toy. He couldn't think of any use for it as there were no paths to pull the thing. It would have been more of a nuisance than anything else. But now they could use it. He only hoped that it was strong enough to hold the wood stove.

The four men headed back to the site dragging the small wagon. In no time at all they loaded the stove and the stove pipe onto the small four-wheeled toy and hoped that the weight wouldn't ruin the tires. But so far it was working well. One man pushed the wagon, one man pulled and two men cleared the way. They traded off now and then to give each a rest but it wasn't too long before a wood stove was positioned in the camp.

Immediately, Peter built a fire in the new addition to the camp. They all had a good laugh. Not too many campers actually had a wood stove in their camp area. They had to use an outside fire and had quite a time getting things set level on the fire so they wouldn't spill. This was going to make cooking so much better. Peter could think of all kinds of things he could cook now that there was an oven.

"Where do you think it came from, Eric?" Bethany asked.

"Well, there was evidence that someone lived there at one time. If we were to be here for a long time, it would be good to walk all over the island and see if anyone is still here, but we haven't found any signs other than what we found by the skeletons. We could have neighbors and not even know it," Eric answered.

"Eric, do you think we should start the engine again and try the radio just in case someone might hear our broadcast and call the airline company?" Albert asked.

"Yes, let's try that airplane's radio while you have it running. I don't think the radio will work if the engine isn't gunning. It doesn't work completely but if we could get it to stay on long enough to say flight 509 someone should hear us and perhaps report that fact to the American government."

Peter walked into the airplane and started it up and then walked back out. "How long should we let it run this time?" he asked.

"Let's try the radio for fifteen minutes. It looks as if we have fixed it but it is iffy. It cuts in and out so we have to try enough to at least get flight 509 broadcasted. We sure don't want to run it too long and run out of gas before they find us," Eric suggested.

"I think fifteen minutes won't use up too much gas," Albert agreed.

"All right, that's what we'll do. You and Peter take care of starting and I'll try the radio," Eric said. That did make sense. An hour might use up too much fuel. Eric knew that even if someone heard the 509 call that they hoped to make, they were on some remote island where planes never go anywhere close to it and the searchers wouldn't know where to search.

He hoped that those looking for them think beyond that the direction to Europe. If they were trying to trace the 509 flight plan they would never come near this island. The pilot only landed here because he had no other choice unless he went into the ocean. He couldn't have seen the island but headed in this direction hoping there would be one.

Eric tried saying flight 509 a few times when they could tell the radio was broadcasting but they knew it didn't work as it should. There was a loose connection somewhere. They finally called it quits for the day.

An hour later the group wanted to turn on the foreign radio again and hear the news. It was about the time that the news came on the last few days. So after the airplane engine was shut off, they turned on the radio and everyone sat down to listen.

First there were some advertisements. They listened to that and knew that the news should come on right after that.

Then they heard the news of what was happening in the United States. Nothing appeared to be too important. They named several criminal events that happened. It would be nice if once in a while they mentioned something good, Bethany thought. But when the new caster mentioned flight 509 everyone sat up and listened carefully.

"We have had just received a notice from some radio operator who claims he heard someone broadcasting flight 509. That's all they were saying and the radio kept going in and out as if it had a short in it. Now if this is coming from survivors on Flight 509 keep it up. Although search planes have looked several times they could find no evidence of a downed airplane. We still can't find the exact location as to where it might have crashed. But we wondered if the survivors had a radio and were listening to this news broadcast. If so, the tower would like you to start the engine now and try the radio once again. We'll know that you listened to this news broadcast every day at this time. We'll keep you informed as to what is going on concerning your rescue."

Peter ran to the airplane and started the motor. Eric worked with the radio again broadcasting the flight 509 for fifteen minutes. Tomorrow they would know if anyone heard them.

After they had turned the engine off the last time, they continued to listen to the newscaster. He seemed so shook up he could hardly talk. The man was happy. "Friends, the people who survived the airplane crash of 509 have done exactly what we ask them to do. Now that we know we can give them instructions, we should be able to find them. This is good news. We have no idea how many survived from the 30 passengers that took the flight, but at least we know some of them did."

While they were sitting around the camp fire that evening, every one of the survivors was pleased over the newscast. Everyone was trying to talk at once. They no longer felt isolated from the rest of the world. They really didn't need to walk all the way to the top of the mountain to see if their cell phones worked. They had a way of telling any rescuers just where they were if the radio did broadcast long enough to do that.

"It looks as though we're going to have to have another celebration after hearing that news. What can we cook that would help us celebrate?" Bethany asked.

"Well, if I just had some string and a hook, I'd catch us a fish. That would be a nice change," Dennis replied.

"Well, there are some fishing things on the shelves in our shelter. I think there is line, hooks, sinker and a reel," Bethany remarked. "We found them in one of the suitcases and thought we might be able to use the line for something so we put them on one of the shelves in the shelter. Come take a look at the things we found. It would be great if you could catch a fish."

Dennis hurried into the shelter. Sure enough everything was there that Bethany had mentioned. He found it a little strange that there wasn't a pole of some kind. "Are you sure there wasn't any fishing pole with this?"

"Oh, there was a funny looking folding stick," Bethany answered and pick up the strange item.

Dennis grinned. "That, my dear, is a fishing pole." He unfolded it and put the reel on it. The reel already had plenty of line. He put a sinker and a hook on the line and then went to find an angle worm. He had seen some one day and teased the girls about cooking angle worms when they ran out of meat. That wasn't the wisest suggestion he'd ever given them and they totally rejected it. They even made faces at him. He knew it was a gross suggestion but once in a while he had to pull their chain and once in a while he had to have a good laugh.

In only a few minutes he had a worm on his hook and headed right where the airplane used to be. Everyone held their breath as he threw the line into the water. In only a few minutes Dennis was pulling in a fish. It was a good size salmon.

All the onlookers were cheering. They would have salmon steaks for breakfast since Bethany and Leslie already were working on the dinner.

"Couldn't we eat that salmon while it is fresh," Dennis asked. "I can catch another one in the morning. Let Peter cook it and add it to our meal. This is evidently a good place to catch salmon and we sure don't have any competition with other fishermen. At least this area hasn't been fished out."

Peter took the big fish, cleaned it and began to cook it. Bethany and Leslie almost had the dinner ready but they would wait a little while longer for the salmon. It sounded absolutely delicious. They watched as Peter put different herbs on the fish. The smell made them all hungry for fish.

"Why didn't you go fishing before?" Jim asked.

"I didn't know that I had fishing equipment available," Dennis replied. "There has to be a river somewhere around here as these salmon are heading there to spawn."

"You're right," Jim agreed.

They soon sat down for their dinner. "Oh, this tastes so good," Eric remarked.

"Yes," everyone agreed. What a nice change of menu.

In the morning, Dennis caught another big fish and they enjoyed salmon steaks for breakfast. It was nice to have such a variety of meat. They had their dried venison, fresh rabbit and now salmon. They had eaten all of the venison that they had stored in fat to keep from spoiling. They sure were eating well for a bunch of people who were stranded on an island, Eric thought.

What was really nice for the cooks was the wood stove. It made it so much easier to cook on it than on a wood fire alone. Now it would be much easier to cook their meals. Even though they may be rescued any day, it was still worth all the work they did to carry the stove to the campsite. They still made a fire at night to sit around and visit. It was a time of comradeship and a time when they learned a lot about one another.

They kept trying to get Jim to tell them what he did for a living. He would just smile and tell them to guess. Only Leslie and Eric had figured it out. He would have thought that by telling them he'd lose his friends, they would have guessed easily what he did for a living. But they didn't.

It was fun to see them trying so hard to think what his occupation was. Some of the strange types of work they came up with were laughable. No, he wasn't a veterinarian and neither was he a taxidermist and he certainly wasn't a pan handler. He was absolutely not a federal tax examiner. At that suggestion, Jim really broke into laughter.

"If one of you were a tax examiner, I'd sure stay away from you," Jim declared. He was sure he liked his job much better than if he'd been a tax examiner.

"If you can't discover my occupation by the time we're rescued, I may tell you and again I may not," Jim stated and smiled. This was a very curious group who just couldn't stand it because he wouldn't tell them what he did for a living. All they had to do was think a little and he was sure it would come to him. Leslie was probably right. He really didn't look like what people pictured an undertaker would look.

"Well, we can always pressure Leslie into telling us," Albert suggested with a smirk of a smile on his face.

"Oh, no," Leslie exclaimed. "I'm not telling anyone. I know how to keep secrets. And this is a good one to keep."

"Well, Bethany is a good friend of yours. I bet you've told her what Jim's occupation is. We could get that information out of Bethany a lot easier than Leslie," Dennis suggested.

"Sorry, Dennis, but Leslie won't even tell me. She said it was for that very reason she wouldn't tell me. She knew I might break down and tell. So I don't know any more about Jim than the rest of you. I just can't picture him in some occupation that we'd all object to."

"Well, kids, it is bedtime," Eric announced. "Maybe during the night you'll dream about an occupation for him.

"Yeah, I'm sure that will happen," Dennis remarked sarcastically.

But they all agreed it was bed time. Every night they went to bed about the same time and all of them were beginning to feel a little sleepy.

CHAPTER 17

A Little Disappointment

The next morning the survivors were eager to get out of bed and ready to eat another meal cooked on the wood stove. It made it easier to cook the pancakes. Sometimes when they cooked over the fire alone they would lose some of the pancakes into the burning ashes. Now they didn't have to worry about that. It sure made cooking a lot more enjoyable, thought Bethany.

Everyone was up and out of bed ready for breakfast except for Jim. Eric wondered about him. He was always one of the first ones up in the morning. He would wait until they all ate and then he would go check on him. So very unusual for him to sleep in, as he had told Eric that he was an early riser. But everyone deserved to sleep in from time to time.

After the breakfast, Eric entered Jim's area. The man was still asleep but he looked very red. He touched the sick man's fore head and knew he had a very high fever. Now what could have brought that on? He tried to shake Jim gently.

The man groaned. "Go away and let me sleep. I'm sick. What ever you want me to do will have to wait until I feel better."

"Jim, you have a high fever. I need to give you some aspirin immediately," Eric exclaimed.

"It won't do any good but you can get me some anyway," Jim answered sleepily and with a weak voice. He turned over and groaned again. He hurt so much that he just wanted to go back to sleep. Couldn't they just leave him alone and let him suffer in peace. There was nothing they could do for him he was quite sure.

Eric walked out to where the rest were talking. "Jim is very sick. I'm giving him a couple of aspirins. He murmured something about it not doing any good. Now it's very unlikely that he has the flu. You usually have to be in touch with someone with the flu to catch it. No one else is sick. I'm open to suggestions. Think about it while I give him the aspirins and wipe his face down with cool water," Eric hurried back to Jim's bed and helped him take the two aspirins.

"Do you know what is wrong with you?" Eric asked while he wiped his forehead with a cool cloth trying to bring down the fever. It's not good for him to have such a high fever for very long. He would guess that it was at least 104 degrees and perhaps even higher.

"Yes," Jim answered and immediately fell back to sleep.

Dennis walked into the room. "Eric, Jim and I have done a lot of things together and I've gotten pretty well acquainted with him. Now he told me a lot about himself and one of the things was that he had a terrible allergy to peanuts. It would make him deathly sick if he ate any. We're still eating those candy bars. If I was guessing I'd say that Jim got a hold of one of the candy bars that had peanuts in it. He probably didn't check the label. Sometimes they grind up the peanuts and you don't realize that there are peanuts in the candy bar," Dennis explained. He sure didn't like the look on his friend's face.

"I believe there's an allergy remedy in the medical kit. Let me go get it real quick before he gets worse. We sure don't want to lose him. He must have eaten it just before he went to bed last night. At least that would be my guess. Otherwise he would have been sick yesterday," Eric stated.

He found the allergy medicine and administered the shot. Then Eric stood back and watched.

"Hey, he looks better already, Eric. Look, his face isn't quite so red. I believe you just saved the man's life. When you get back home, you better work on getting your doctor degree," Dennis suggested.

"No thanks. I couldn't take the pressure. Do you know what this did to me? I'll probably have a nightmare tonight over this. I could never stand to be a doctor. Being a medic is a close as I want to get. I'm only a medic because that was one of the requirements at my dad's factory. They had to have a medic in the building. A woman and I were chosen. I thought it would be a snap and rather fun, but I've changed my mind since," Eric exclaimed.

Albert and Peter came into the shelter to see how Jim was. "He's much better thanks to Dr. Eric. He evidently had a candy bar with peanuts in it and he's very allergic to them. He probably just ate it and didn't read the ingredients. I bet he doesn't make that mistake again," Dennis remarked.

They all left Jim sleeping. He seemed to be in a deep sleep. He probably didn't get much sleep last night with his allergies bothering him. They'd just wait and let Jim get up when he decided that he felt well enough. The group had eaten their breakfast and was ready for another day of work. There was always something to do, Peter thought. But he knew that was a good thing.

People would be bored to tears if they didn't have something to do. Bethany couldn't stand it very long when they didn't let her help with the work. It made her restless. If there wasn't anything to do, they'd have a camp full of restless people. No, it was a good thing to stay busy. Eric had been a good leader for all of them in that he always had a task for them to do.

The two ladies were off looking for food. Eric wanted Albert and Peter to work on making the inside of the airplane into a home. He suggested that they turn the seats up against the wall as to look like a couch. But the other seats they needed to break down into beds. It should be easy when they lean back a seat, just to break it all together and it would fall back to the next seat and make a bed.

Albert and Peter got right to work. "We'll make a room in the back for the two girls. I suggest that we let them use the toilet facilities in there. I'll fix it so it can be emptied easily," Albert exclaimed.

Eric nodded his head. Albert wanted things to be nice for Bethany. That was all right. This would keep those two busy for quite a while.

"Well, since Jim is sick, how about catching another big fish for us?" Eric asked Dennis.

"You never have to ask me twice if I want to go fishing. That was a hobby of mine. It would be nice to have a little more of those salmon steaks on the menu today," Dennis replied. "I promised Jim he could do the fishing this morning, but since he's sick, I'll get one for you."

The two went to look for worms and picked up about three of the wiggly creatures and headed to the open beach area. Dennis threw the line way out into the water. It wasn't long before he had a fish on the hook and he reeled it in.

"Look at that," he quipped. "I guess everyone around here knows that Dennis Williams is one of the best fishermen one could ask for."

"It must be a pretty good salmon hole for someone to throw a line out and in less than two or three minutes have a salmon on the line. Yes, Dennis, we know you're a great fisherman and we are grateful for the big fish you have caught for us." Eric smiled. Leave it to Dennis to make a big thing about it so he could bring in a laugh or two as easily as he did the salmon. It was rather nice to have a comic in the group.

"What do you think this is, Dr. Eric? It's not beginners luck as I'm no beginner when it comes to fishing."

Eric just laughed and went to check on Jim. When he entered Jim's portion of the shelter, he noticed that he was sitting up.

"You feeling a little better now," Jim," Eric asked.

"Oh, a whole lot better, believe me. I wanted to tell you what was wrong with me but I couldn't stay awake long enough. I shouldn't have eaten that candy bar. I'll have to read the ingredients on the wrappings after this. Boy, did I feel awful. I felt that I was dying and I hurt so much that I just didn't care if I did. I was having a hard time trying to breathe. But I feel great now. That extra sleep was rather nice," Jim replied.

"I'm glad you're okay. You had us worried, my friend," Eric stated.

"Did I hear something about someone pulling in another salmon? Dennis was going to let me do the fishing today. You get sick one day and you lose your job. I was sure I could bring in one of those big salmon. At least I sure wanted to try," Jim grinned. It was nice to have salmon and it didn't matter who caught it.

"You sure had us worried. You can thank Dennis for telling us that you had allergies and was allergic to peanuts. I'd never have guessed what to do with you if he hadn't told me. At any rate, I'm glad that you're up and around now."

It was time to listen to the broadcast again. Although they listened to the whole program, they weren't mentioned. That made about three days in a row that they didn't make the news. Surely they hadn't given up on finding them. They were worried that the batteries in the radio were going to quit. There were no battery chargers anywhere to be found. Eric began to worry. Why didn't the radio mention them? Why didn't they give them some more instructions as to what to do? Perhaps they had better start thinking of another plan of rescue.

The news had been broadcasting everything for a week and now nothing. He walked over to Albert. "Do you suppose we should start the engine again and try broadcasting over the radio our simple flight 509 message so they know we are still alive and well? I can't figure out why they haven't mentioned us for three days. It doesn't make any sense to me, does it to you?"

"No, except they just don't have anything to report. But because we haven't been trying the radio since we heard their broadcast, I think it would be a good idea to run it now. You just don't know what to think. They may have thought it was some pranksters and yet they should have known the radio message was coming from the airplane that crashed. I'll have Pilot Peter start up the engine," Albert remarked with a twinkle in his eyes. He loved to tease Peter.

Peter overhead the conversation and headed for the airplane. He too thought it was a good idea to start the engine and play with the airplane's radio. They were a disappointed group when no other mention of them was heard on the foreign radio. Peter let it run for fifteen minutes and then quit while Eric tried to send messages. If they could just find out where the loose wires were but when they looked at it, it seemed fine but their messages sure broke up. Perhaps tomorrow would bring some remarks over the foreign radio broadcast about flight 509.

They realized the newscast was over and they'd have to wait until tomorrow to see if their signal brought any response. As excited as that newsman was when he first heard some one report they heard 509 over their radio, they couldn't belief that he no longer mentioned them.

Eric called the group together. "Let's work a little harder on trying to broadcast on that foreign radio," he suggested.

"That's a good idea," Leslie stated. "We rather forgot to keep working at it. Tomorrow, we'll try it again. I sure hope the news mentions us again. It seems so strange that they'd forget us so quickly."

"I know," Eric said. "You'd think they'd say something like they couldn't locate us. Just something but to absolutely ignore us doesn't make much sense. We just have to be patient with them. Perhaps they are working on the problem and just don't have anything to report as yet."

"That's probably it. They had their audience all excited and then since they couldn't find us, they didn't want to report anything more. Perhaps tomorrow they will since Peter did the same thing this time with the engine as the newscaster had asked him," Jim exclaimed. He hadn't given up hope.

"I wonder if we should try something else. Perhaps we should walk to the top of the mountain and try out our cell phones again. We don't have to just stay with one thing. They may well be on their way or they may be trying to find out where we are," Eric suggested.

"I think that would be a good idea," Jim agreed.

"I wouldn't mind another walk to the top of the mountain. Maybe we'd find another deer," Dennis exclaimed.

"That would be nice," Bethany remarked. With the spices they had put on the deer steaks, they tasted just like regular steaks. She and Leslie had really enjoyed them and wouldn't mind having some more.

CHAPTER 18

A Surprise Hurricane

That evening just before the sun set the group felt a strong wind blowing. It kept getting a little stronger as the time passed. It wasn't particularly cold but it was very strong and they had to fight to stand up. Eric had been in hurricane weather before and he was afraid that this wind was getting close to hurricane speed.

"Everyone head for the airplane. This wind looks as though it might be turning into a hurricane. The shelter will never hold up to it. Hurry, let's get into the airplane. Be sure and bring the radio and anything else that's important to us. Perhaps you better grab your bedding as well," Eric suggested.

Everyone grabbed blanket, food, water and anything else they could think of and walked up the steps into the airplane. By this time, Peter and Albert had the beds ready and the seats turned to form living room couches. They even put a blanket up between the ladies bedroom and the men's.

Everyone was surprised when they stepped into the airplane and saw what Peter and Albert had accomplished. It looked like an apartment. They were pleased.

The wind didn't even seem to rock the airplane at all but it was doing some havoc to their shelter. Eric wished they would have had time to put the stove into the airplane and then they would have a fire but it was too late now. It was unlikely that the wind would hurt the stove in anyway. Perhaps tomorrow they would move the stove into the airplane. He was quite sure they couldn't live in the shelter anymore.

"I think we should all turn in now that the beds are made. We better work on making this comfortable as I don't think the shelter is going to be of much use to us anymore," Eric explained.

"How about just a couple of songs from our harmonica player first," Leslie asked. She looked at Eric with pleading eyes.

"That might be a good idea. We don't have the fire place to sit around but let's have some music before we head for bed," Eric agreed.

They sang several songs. Jim always included one or two hymns as they were his favorite type of songs. Finally, Jim put the harmonica away and the group headed for bed.

It was much earlier than when they usually retired but there wasn't much else to do. There was no fire to sit around and visit and the plane was getting a little chilly. The blankets were going to feel good.

Eric noticed that most of the people didn't say too much. He was probably the only one that had ever been in a hurricane and he was sure they had heard terrible things that hurricanes did to houses and people. He watched the worried looks on their faces. They did follow his suggestions and headed for bed.

"Folks, although this is probably hurricane strength, I'm sure we are going to be just fine. God has taken care of us all these weeks and He will continue to do so. Go to bed and just try to get some sleep."

So the two girls went into the back of the airplane and made ready for bed. They liked their new room. And the beds were pretty comfortable. At least it was a lot cleaner than the shelter because the walls were clean as well as the floor. Yes, this was a good bedroom they both decided.

It wasn't long before everyone was sleeping except Eric. He had moved away from hurricane country as he had lost friends in one of the terrible storms. He began to pray for his group that God would take care of them. At least they appeared safe in the airplane as the strong winds didn't move the airplane at all. He thanked the Lord for watching over all of them.

When morning came, Eric was the first one up. He quietly stepped out of the plane and looked around. The shelter was in shambles. Things were thrown all over everywhere. Well, he knew what they would all be doing to keep busy today and probably the next couple of days. At least the stove was there. He built a fire in it. He found the pan where they boiled the water. It was quite some distance away from the stove. So he cleaned it and put the water on to boil. Everyone would want some herb tea right off.

He wasn't a cook so he didn't want to start breakfast. Now if they had eggs, bacon, and bread with a toaster, he would be right at home but grinding roots for flour to make pancakes wasn't down his alley. He had a sack of ready mix pancake flour at home when he wanted the flat cakes. He didn't have any idea what they would put in the pancakes besides the ground roots.

He heard a noise and looked up to see Bethany staring at the shelter. "Can we get our food storage out of there?" she asked. "We worked hard on that and I'd hate to see it wasted." She wiped a tear out of her eyes. She knew it was silly to be so upset since God had taken care of them and no one was hurt. But she and Leslie had worked hard on the food storage for winter and she sure wanted to rescue it.

"I'm sure we can, Bethany. When everyone has breakfast we'll move all the logs and stuff out of the shelter and retrieve all the things we want and take them into the airplane. There are plenty of storage places above the seats. That will make good cupboards. Now tell me what you need to cook breakfast this morning," Eric asked her.

"Well, I thought when I saw all of this that we ought to get out the energy bars and juice drinks and call it breakfast. I don't know where the pan is that I usually cook with nor the big tin that I use as a frying pan. What do you think? Can we just have the energy bars?"

"Bethany, after the stove cools off, we are going to move it into the airplane and put the stove pipe on it. It will keep us warm. It's getting a little colder and after that wind last night, it just might be that this is the windy season. I thank God that we have that airplane to use as shelter," Eric exclaimed.

"You're right. I don't know how we'd stay warm on the airplane if cold weather came without that woodstove. Let's see if we can find that suitcase that has the energy bars in it. We didn't empty it completely. That looks like it right there with that little tree lying across it."

Eric rescued the suitcase and sure enough the energy bars and some juice drinks were in there. The two decided to go ahead and eat. They made themselves some hot herbal tea to go with the bars and juice.

One by one the others came out and joined them. Each one groaned when they saw what the strong wind had done to their shelter. After everyone had eaten, they began to work on moving all the poles and things that obstructed the way into the shelter. As soon as everything was cleared, they each entered and carried things they needed into the airplane. Without a roof, that shelter was of no use. Even one of the walls was missing.

Bethany and Leslie headed for their food storage and took all that they could carry into the plane. It took several trips before they moved their food storage out of the cellar and onto the airplane.

They saw some of the suitcases that they had opened to dry out were thrown all over everywhere along with the contents. They all worked together to bring the suitcases and belongings back to their area. At this point they didn't want to put the wet suitcases into the plane so they hoped the sun would dry them out before another windstorm came.

At noon they all took a break and had some of Bethany's rabbit stew. They were tired already and still had the afternoon to go. It hadn't been one of the better days that they had during their stay on the island.

Eric talked with Albert about something and he thought was a good possibility. He didn't want to tell everyone what he was planning. He wanted it to be a surprise.

As soon as the stove cooled off, the men carried it into the plane and made a whole in the roof for the stove pipe. Their stack of wood was scatter all over and that was another thing they had to gather up. They decided that the luggage department was a good place to store dry suitcases, wood, and anything else they might possibly need. They still wanted to save whatever they hadn't used out of the suitcases for relatives of the passengers who hadn't lived. Dennis made a door to put over the whole they had made in the luggage compartment. It was easy to open and get into the compartment that way and it also protected the contents of the luggage department. They sure didn't need any rain water getting into that area and getting everything wet.

Once the stove was located in the airplane, Eric built a fire in it. It sure warmed the plane in a hurry. He knew they would have to keep the fire down a little or it would be too warm for them in their new home.

Eric watched as Bethany and Leslie carefully placed the dishes and food in certain places. They were very methodical in what they did. They wanted to know exactly where everything was. The group had almost forgotten that they were on the island. After not hearing for a few days, they seemed to feel it would be quite a while before they'd be rescued.

That would be all right now that they had their home in the airplane. It was warm, clean and comfortable. They could wait a little longer for someone to come and rescue them.

CHAPTER 19

A Test of the Spanish Language

Eric suggested that at least every other day they start the engine up and try to get the radio to send out a message. At least someone would be getting the message. It was almost time for the broadcast and they hoped they could hear some good news for a change.

"It appears we are still hearing from our survivors on Flight 509. The supervisors are beginning to think that the messages are real and not someone trying to send out fake flight 509 information to get their attention. Once again, the airline officials are going to make every effort to locate the surviving crew of Flight 509. When the airlines tried to fly the route that 509 would have taken, they found no islands in the region. It hasn't been easy to try to find the location of the crash.

"If the survivors would keep sending the radio message while the airplane motor is allowing it to for five minutes that would be sufficient enough for them to search for the island they're on. It's apparent that the survivors could run out of gas so it suggested that they only let it run for five minutes only. If you have any other method of contacting us, please do so. There usually are cell phones, or some type of Morse code equipment. Do everything you can to contact someone in the states.

"That's all the news we have today for Flight 509. Now for other news..."

At that point, they turned the radio off. They sure needed to find someway to charge the radio battery although Albert did note that it was a good sized battery and it would last quite some time. He was sure the owner would have charged the battery before taken on the flight.

As Eric thought things over, he decided that perhaps it might be a good idea now to have someone walk to the top of the mountain again and this time with a cell phone. All the phones had been charged and some of the batteries had been removed. He hated to ask Dennis and Jim to walk up there again, but it appeared to be necessary.

"You're doing some deep thinking, Dr. Eric. What's on your mind? I have an idea that you want Dennis and me to walk to the top of the mountain in the morning and try out Albert's cell phone. Am I right?" Jim asked.

"Now I know what you do for a living. You're a mind reader," Eric remarked and grinned. It was just the logical thing to do and Jim knew it.

"We'll go early in the morning. We'll pack a lunch. I think there is some more of those health and candy bars but I'm going to read the label this time. I don't want to take a chance in eating any more peanuts. Is it all right with you, Albert, if we take your cell phone up to the top of the mountain and see what happens?" Jim asked.

"Sure but let me show you a few things about it. It's a lot more than an ordinary cell phone and it picks up signals where other plain cell phones don't. Let me give you a quick lesson. Everyone is busy cleaning up the hurricane mess so this will get us both out of a little work," Albert remarked and grinned.

"Yes, we've all been working a little too hard to clean up this mess. Bethany still hasn't found her fry pan as she called it. It was so light weight there is no telling where it might be. Since it was just a piece of tin, it went flying with the winds I'm sure. It's too bad about the shelter as it was rather nice to have even though we have better shelter now. Okay, how do you work this thing?" Jim asked.

Albert went into a lot of detail that Jim thought was unnecessary. But soon he began to understand why Albert was telling him all this information. If one thing didn't work, another might. There were several options and different things to do depending on what the distance was. Yes, it was all making sense now. Leave it to this engineer to have a complicated and sophisticated cell phone and a complicated way of telling one how to use it. But right now he was thankful that Albert had an exceptional one.

They by no means had the results of the hurricane cleared up. It would take several days. Eric suggested that they go at it a little slower pace. He had looked at the tired faces. Everyone seemed to be exhausted. There wasn't any hurry since they found their food and most of their cooking utensils.

"Let's retire early tonight," Eric suggested.

No one objected. They went into the airplane and sat down. After Bethany and Leslie had fixed the evening meal, Peter told them that he and Albert had a surprise for them. Albert went over to the movie screen and pulled it down. Then he pushed some buttons and a movie began to play.

Everyone shouted. "This is great." It was a movie they had all seen before but they rather enjoyed seeing it again. It was almost like being in civilization again. Once the movie was finished they sat in their "living room" and visited. They talked about Jim and Dennis' trip to the top of the mountain. They hoped and prayed Albert's cell phone would reach someone.

The next morning, Jim and Dennis prepared for their trip to the top of the mountain. Everyone watched as they ascended the path they had made before.

The one fear that was in the back of the mind of each survivor was that the airplane would run out of gas and they'd have no way to signal for help. They had to get the cell phone to work or the foreign radio one. Eric began to think about that strange radio again. It sure would be a plus if they could figure out a way to reach someone that they could talk with about rescuing them.

"Albert, how did you and Leslie make out with that foreign radio? Did you even get close to making it work?" Eric asked.

"Yes we did but then things happened and we had to put it away. But now that the bulk of the hurricane mess is cleaned up, I think we shall go back to working on it. Leslie, where did you put that radio?"

Leslie brought it out and they put it on their makeshift table and the two began to work on it. "If any one else has any suggestions, we would appreciate your input. We can hear some radio programs on it but the instructions for using it as a two way radio is all written in a foreign language. Does anyone know a few words in French or Spanish, or some other language than English that we might try to read these instructions?" Leslie waited for an answer.

Everyone came over and took a look at the words. "Well that word there means push or press in a lot of languages," Dennis remarked.

"Well, that word means one in Spanish. Uno, dos, tres... Are there any more words that sound like numbers?" Jim asked.

"Yes, cinco is five isn't it?" Peter asked.

"I wonder if this might be in Spanish. But I understand French is similar to the Spanish language," Eric commented.

"So the words on the buttons are actually numbers," Albert said slowly. "That gives us a little clue. Now look at the instructions.

Between all of them they managed to figure out a few of the words in the instruction booklet. It appeared that you had to push cinco and uno at the same time if you wanted to do something but what? It was worth a try. They turned the radio on and then pushed both buttons and talked into the mike. "May day, May day," Albert said and released the lever.

"Que es su nombre?" a voice asked.

"Doesn't that mean what is your name?" asked Leslie.

Albert pushed the lever again and said, "Albert. We crashed in Flight 509." He figured that everyone in the world had probably heard about that flight by now.

"Feeve O Neene. Crash. Si senor. No habla Ingles." He let up on the speaker.

"No habla Espanol," Albert responded. "Habla to America. We're stranded. Can you help us?" Albert let go.

"No habla Ignles. Uno momento," the voice said.

"That means wait a minute or a moment. Perhaps they have someone who knows a little bit of Ingles and they are getting that person. Let's hope and pray," Albert commented.

Eric was shocked at Albert's words but said nothing. Being around a group of Christians had rather rubbed off on him. In about cinco momentos the voice came back on the phone.

"Are you survivors of Flight 509?" he asked.

"Yes and are we happy that you can speak English. We need you to get a hold of someone in America and tell them our position if you know where we are. We have seven survivors waiting to be rescued," Albert explained.

"I'll call immediately. We have your general location noted by our GPS system so hang in there. It may take some time, but you'll be rescued. Have you anything to eat?" he asked.

"There's plenty on this island to eat if you're industrious enough to find it. We have plenty of food, water and shelter. But we'd still like to be rescued so we can return to our homes."

"I'll call you back as soon as I reach the American authorities. This may take some time. It could be tomorrow before I get through to them. May God take care of you, my friends." With this comment, the man hung up.

"Why didn't I ask him his name?" Albert remarked disgustingly.

"You did fine, Albert. We don't need to know the man's name. I'm sure that he'll start working on our problem immediately. He sure appeared eager to help us. Now we can relax and wait for him to call back," Eric said.

"I'm sure pleased that we all put our heads together to figure out that foreign manual," Leslie stated.

"Together we managed to figure it out. Now I hope the battery isn't too weak to receive the message he said he would give us after contacting the American officials," Albert remarked.

"We really haven't used it all that much. Don't you suppose the man would have a fresh battery in it if he was taking it somewhere to use?" Eric asked.

"Yeah, it should be fine. When I get back home, I'm sure going to study Spanish. I might even take a class in it," Albert remarked.

"Yes, I'd like to do that too," Bethany stated and Leslie agreed. It wouldn't hurt to know another language in case something like this happened again. But they hoped it wouldn't happen again, once in their life time was enough.

They could hardly wait to tell Jim and Dennis the good news.

CHAPTER 20

Finding Bears

Since the radio had reached the desired destination and the promise of help would soon be on the way, Leslie and Bethany decided to make another trip to gather more berries, roots or whatever they could find. They wanted to go a little further this time than they had before. It was still fairly early and they should be back in time to start the lunch.

When they reached the usual food gathering spot, they picked some berries as they just couldn't resist. They passed on by and walked about another quarter of a mile. Then they stopped suddenly. They stared at what they saw. Bears! The two quietly walked back toward the camp. They didn't dare run as bears figured you were bait if you ran from them. Leslie remembered that from her wilderness training.

They just prayed that the bears hadn't noticed them but Leslie knew that their scent would be picked up easily by the bears and especially the one closest to them. The wind was blowing right toward them and onto the bears. The two hurried as fast as they could. They looked back and saw one bear leisurely following them. They walked faster. They really wanted to run but they knew the bear could out run them very easily and if they ran the bear would run after them.

As the bear gained on them, Leslie told Bethany to throw down her berries. "The bear will take time to eat that before coming after us."

Bethany sadly emptied her beautiful berries in the middle of the path and hurried on down toward the camp. They were getting close to the camp and decided that it would probably be okay to run now that the bear was busy eating the berries. Both girls ran as fast as they could. They reach camp as the bear was only a short distance away from them. He had seen them running and was coming after them.

Albert looked up and decided that the bear might catch up with the two frightened girls. He picked up a club and stepped between Bethany and the bear. Leslie ran into the airplane and pulled Bethany in after her.

The girls were yelling now to get the attention of Eric and Peter. Albert needed help and quickly. Both girls were crying as they saw the bear attack their friend.

Albert was doing all he could with his club to keep the bear away from him. Eric and Peter each picked up a club and headed for the bear but by that time Albert was down on the ground and the bear was mauling him.

Eric was sick to his stomach. Both men hit the bear with all the strength that they had. Eric used his makeshift knife and cut the bear's throat as Peter wacked him with all his strength. The cut wasn't enough to kill the animal. The bear was unconscious and the two men kept hitting him hoping they could kill him. He had one tough head. Eric finally picked up a big rock and smashed it into the bear's head and then cut his throat some more.

When they were certain that the bear was dead, they picked up Albert and carried him into the plane and placed him on his bed.

"Peter, you take care of that bear. It would make some good steaks and Bethany and I will take care of Albert. Leslie, would you help Peter however he needs you?" Eric suggested.

Both girls went right to work still shedding tears over the incident. Leslie took one last look at Albert and shook her head. He looked terrible with all that blood and scratches on his face.

Eric carefully took off Albert's shirt and washed the wounds and put some disinfectant on them. His arms and face seemed to have the worst punctures. Bethany was putting on the ointment and the bandage on the wounds. Eric wished that Albert would moan or move when he cleaned and disinfected the wounds. But Albert never moved an inch. He was completely unaware of what they were doing to him.

"You know he did this for me," Bethany exclaimed. "He stepped right in between the bear and me. The bear would have mauled me if he hadn't done that," Bethany cried with tears falling down her cheeks.

"I know I saw him step between you and the bear. It took a lot of guts to do that. He's a brave man."

"Albert, Albert can you hear me," Bethany asked.

No response.

"I imagine he's in shock. So far I haven't found any of the punctures that have excessive bleeding. But Bethany, we have to keep after these wounds as they can easily become infected. So even when he awakes and argues that he doesn't need all this attention, you have to convince him otherwise." Eric explained this to Bethany trying to make her see what needed to be done and not dwell on what that bear did. He also knew Albert just enough to know that he'd think he didn't need all that medical care on the wounds. Bethany would have to convince him otherwise and he was quite sure the man wouldn't argue with Bethany.

Eric sure hated to see the bear punctures on the face but at least they weren't that deep. In fact they looked more like claw marks on the face and bite marks on the arms. So perhaps his face wouldn't be scared.

"How did it happen that you ran across bears? The whole time we've been here you and Leslie never saw a bear before."

"We wanted to see what was further on than our usual place where we got berries and other items. When we saw all the bears we carefully started back hoping that the bears didn't notice us, but the wind was blowing right toward them and I imagine the bears smelled our scent. At least the one closest to us did. Eric, there were lots of bears, believe me. It's a wonder more bears didn't follow us back to camp," Bethany answered.

"They still could. We all have to be on the alert and watch for the animals. We need to pray that our two men don't run into any bears where they're going. It seems that most of the animals with the exception of the rabbits are located further east. And the deer they caught was up around the top of the peak. Perhaps the bears don't go there."

When Eric finished treating all of the facial and the arm wounds, he remarked, “Bethany, I’m going to take off Albert’s pants and make sure his legs or bottom don’t have bear punctures. His pants are torn and I don’t know if he has a bear bite on his legs or not.”

“I’ll step out then,” she suggested and did so.

Eric was pleased that there were no other punctures. Now that Albert had gone into shock, he had to keep him warm and his head slightly up. There was nothing for shock in the medical kit and all he could do from now on was pray for the man. It had to take a lot of guts to run in front of that bear to protect the ladies. Albert had to know that he didn’t have a chance by himself.

Eric suspected that Albert was in love with Bethany. But Bethany was only trying to be a good friend to Albert. He supposed he might have done it for one of the girls and would like to think he would but… He shivered. What an awful thing to have gone through. It was no wonder that the man was in shock.

He put Albert’s pants back on and called Bethany. “We want to lay him down so that his head is higher than the rest of his body. We need to keep him warm. Find some more blankets for me.”

Bethany hurried and soon handed Eric about ten blankets. She didn’t know how many he needed but she wanted to bring plenty.

“Now I need you to talk to him. Whisper to him anything you can to get his attention. He’s more attached to you than anyone else in our group and if anyone can bring him out of this shock condition, you can. If it doesn’t work right away, we’ll wait and try it a little later. In about half an hour I want to try to get him to drink some herbal tea and I’ll need your help. In the meantime, hold his hand and pat it and anything else you can do to help him.”

Bethany picked up Albert’s hand and started stroking it gently. “Albert, this is Bethany. Can you hear me? Try to talk to me. Squeeze my hand if you can.”

No response from Albert.

Eric took out the stethoscope and listened to Albert’s heart beat. It was strong enough. He hadn’t lost that much blood. Evidently, he was just in shock and they had to give him some time to come out of it. In the meantime he thought that perhaps he should give him a shot to ward off infection. He knew there was some penicillin in the medical kit so he grabbed the kit and administered the shot.

Well, thought Eric, if I had gone through that ordeal, I might never come out of a shock condition. I think I might have had a heart attack. That was an awful scene to see and a worse yet to be the victim.

Bethany stayed right by Albert. From time to time she put more medicine on his sores. The last thing the man needed was infected bear bites or claw scratches. She kept talking to him ever so often but was disappointed when he didn't respond. She knew nothing about people who were in shock or what one was supposed to do to help them. She would follow Eric's advice and try to get him to talk.

Eric stepped out of the airplane. There was nothing more he could do to help Albert. He would leave Bethany there to watch him for a while.

Bethany sang a hymn. She thought perhaps a song might soothe him.

Finally, Eric suggested that she just let Albert sleep and for her to come on down and join the rest of them.

She did.

CHAPTER 21

Bear Steaks

The two men came back to camp. They were disappointed. "We couldn't reach anyone, Eric. No signal at all. On top of that we didn't even see a deer. Hey, what's that hanging in the tree? A bear? You killed a bear. Wow, Peter, look what we missed. Not a real big one but big enough to have some bear steaks for dinner," Jim exclaimed very pleased at the idea of steaks.

"It isn't all good news," Leslie exclaimed. "The bear followed Bethany and me to our camp and we ran into the plane. Albert could see that Bethany wasn't going to make it before the bear caught her so he stepped in between the bear and Bethany. If he hadn't the bear would have mauled her. Albert is in bad shape. Eric fixed up his wounds but he's in shock. Eric can't seem to bring him out of it as yet. The bear really mauled him with its paws all over his face and bites on his arms." Leslie's voice had tears in it as she told the returning hikers what happened.

"Oh, that's terrible," Dennis exclaimed. "I want to see him." He hurried into the airplane and looked at Albert. Bethany had returned to see how Albert was doing and tried talking with him again.

Albert began to move a little and groan. Then he settled back down. "Eric tried to get him to drink some tea, but he just wouldn't wake up. I hope he isn't like this too long. I'm worried about him," Bethany exclaimed.

"The shock will go away in time. I imagine that if a bear mauled any one of us, we'd go into shock. But every now and then, you talk to him," Dennis remarked. "It would be nice if he'd wake up by dinner time."

"With all this stuff going on, we just had health bars for lunch along with some juice. We were going to cook when Leslie and I returned, but Eric and I helped clean and bandage his wounds and Leslie and Peter cleaned the bear and skinned it. They're rather proud of their bear skin rug." Bethany smiled for the first time since Albert was hurt.

"Why don't you take a break and come outside? There's not much you can do for him until he gets over this. He could be like this until tomorrow," Dennis suggested. Bethany was looking so weary and tired and he knew it was because she was worried. A little air would do her good.

She walked out of the airplane with him. "Eric, should we just let him sleep now? I can start dinner."

"It's too late, Bethany," Peter remarked. "I already have the steaks on cooking. I finally found your frying pan under some tree limbs. We'll have the steaks and Leslie made a dandelion salad and I'll make some pancakes to eat with the steaks. We're all set for supper. We cooked it outside since Albert was hurt and we didn't want to disturbed him. Believe me cooking on that wood stove is sure a lot easier that what I'm doing now. Bethany, you've been under a strain and I want you to sit down and just watch Leslie and I finish cooking the meal."

Bethany didn't argue. She felt exhausted, totally exhausted. She'd sure be happy when Albert woke up. Eric said his heart beat was good. She would enjoy the steaks more if Albert could eat them too. It just wasn't that long ago that she'd watched her parents die. First one died and then the other, both with heart problems aggravated by the automobile accident. She had to shake this whole idea of death. Albert was going to be fine.

The group heartily ate the bear steaks. They were just finishing up when they heard Albert scream. Eric took two big steps and was in the airplane in nothing flat. Bethany was right behind him. He walked over to the sick man and looked at him. He was fighting the air as if it were the bear.

"Albert," Bethany cried and grabbed his hand. "Albert, you're all right. You're in the airplane. You saved my life. Albert, can you hear me?"

Albert shook his head and looked at her.

"The bear didn't get to you?" he asked.

"Oh, no, Albert, you protected me. You were so brave. I don't know of anyone else that would have done what you did. Are you able to eat? We have bear steaks for dinner."

Albert looked at Bethany and looked at the way she was holding his hand. He smiled at her. "Well, I guess that serves that bear right. He scared the daylight out of us and we'll just eat him out of revenge," he exclaimed and then started to sit up.

"Oh, ouch, oh that hurt. What happened to me?" he asked Bethany.

"You stepped between me and the bear and tried to kill it with your club but that didn't work and the bear mauled you. I was so afraid for you. Peter and Eric killed the bear but not before he did some damage to you. Eric and I fixed your wounds but they're going to hurt for a while. The facial ones are more from the claws, but he did bite your arms. We have to keep them clean and change the bandages twice a day and maybe more," Bethany ordered.

"Sure, we'll do that," he said and grinned. He would love to have Bethany as his nurse and fix his wounds. He had let go of her hand when he tried to get up. He didn't want to groan or complain in front of Bethany so he stood up slowly.

"Albert, let me help you up. It's so good to see you awake. I think you went into shock there for a while. But it's good to see you up and around," Eric exclaimed.

"Oh, I can make it. I'll just use Bethany as a cane and let her help me. She's prettier than you are, Eric," Albert stated.

"I won't argue that," Eric responded with a grin.

Bethany and Albert walked out of the plane together. She dished him up the steak, salad and pancakes and gave him a drink.

"Hey, I like being waited on. I'll see if I can carry this situation on for a few days when I get service like this," he remarked and smiled at Bethany.

"We're all glad that you're conscious, Albert," Jim remarked. "You had us worried there for a while. Eric said you had been out for several hours. You're a little peeked looking so you best let these two ladies wait on you. They're pretty good at that."

Eric looked at Albert. He hadn't noticed it in the plane but the man was pale. That probably had to do with going into shock. He hoped the mauled man felt like eating a good dinner if for no other reason than to please the beautiful Bethany. One thing for sure, Albert would do anything for Bethany. But then, he wasn't the only man in the camp that would do anything the pretty gal asked.

Leslie was a strong and outgoing young woman and all the men liked her, but she didn't need much help. Bethany on the other hand needed to be taken care of and looked after at least that's what Eric thought.

Eric watched Albert and noticed that after he had eaten, his color was better. He still groaned when he moved around but he could expect the sores to hurt him for the next few days.

CHAPTER 22

New Rules

"In all this excitement, we forgot to tell you two men that we did get through on the radio. We got a hold of someone in Spain, we think. At first he said, 'No habla Ingles' and we said, 'No habla Espanol.' But he said, 'Uno momento.' So we waited about five minutes and then a man who spoke English talked with us. He sounded very American but we were so excited about reaching someone that we didn't get his name or ask where he was or anything. All we did was ask him to contact the United States and tell them where we are located. He said his GPS pretty well told him the general direction of our camp. He seemed to know what island we were on," Albert explained.

"No kidding," Jim exclaimed. "You really did reach someone. That's great! Well then we ought to get rescued one of these days. There's going to be a problem and they will find that out when they come. There's no place to land a plane on this island. I don't know about bear country but I wouldn't advice that. Leslie said there were a lot of bears there."

"On top of that, the water isn't deep enough for a ship to get very close to this island. They'll have to bring some smaller boats to rescue us. Isn't that a good word, rescue," Eric commented.

"I like that word," Bethany said and Leslie agreed.

"But regardless how long it takes before we get rescued, we're pretty comfortable and we can wait. I know it will take a while to get a ship here. The rescue will probably be by the military. There aren't a lot of other ships available," Jim commented.

"You're right but we're pretty sure we don't have to spend the winter here even though it's a little colder than when we first came to this island. But, I still think we should keep preparing for the worst and hope and pray for the best. One rule is that the food gatherers shouldn't go east anymore. Head west and take what you can find or go up the hill a ways. But definitely stay completely away from the bears' territory," Eric demanded.

"I think we should do more than that. I think a man ought to go with them and carry a big club." Albert wasn't about to take any more chances with the two ladies running into bears again.

"You mean you think it's going to take a club to get us ladies to do our job? Is that what you think, Albert?" Leslie asked.

Albert just grinned at the ladies. They knew exactly what he was talking about but wanted to tease him a bit. It looked like it hurt him to smile as it affected his sores when he used the muscles to smile.

"How are you doing, Albert? Are you hurting much?" Dennis asked.

"Oh, I'm sore here and there but I heal quickly. In no time at all, my face will be as handsome as it always was." Albert didn't even crack a smile at his comment.

Dennis and Peter burst out laughing. "Oh, he's getting well alright. Just listen to him," Peter remarked. He and Albert had become good friends when they worked on the airplane engine. He sure respected him a lot more than he did at first. Albert had a chip on his shoulder and a big one. But now he was more like the rest of the survivors. Peter decided that he was a very intelligent man and he'd enjoyed working with him on the airplane engine. He sure learned a lot about mechanics.

The survivors went to bed that night a little more excited than they had before. Now they would be rescued for sure but it was just a matter of when.

The first thing that Eric did when he got out of bed the next morning was to check on Albert. The man was much better than he was the day before. Eric watched as Albert ate a good breakfast and moved around much better than he had the day before.

"Now since the hurricane mess is cleaned up, we're a little freer today to do some pleasure walking," Eric announced.

"Well, since the work is done, I want to go on a food hunt with the ladies," Peter exclaimed.

"Me too," Dennis agreed.

"I want to see what is up there as well," Eric said.

"I'm going to stay with Albert," Bethany announced. "I just don't think he should be left alone for a while. You five go looking for food or whatever and we'll watch the camp. We won't be too far from the steps of the plane, though. You can count on that."

Eric agreed that someone should stay with Albert. He said he was alright but that wasn't exactly true. Some of the claw marks were infected. He had to take special care of the bite marks. Albert wasn't ready for an exhausting walk and Eric was glad that Bethany had suggested they stay in the camp.

"Bethany, please put some disinfectant on Albert's sores while we are gone. He needs to do that two or three times a day and don't let him talk you out of doing that," Eric suggested.

Bethany brought the medical kit out of the airplane and began to tend to Albert's wounds. He never said anything to her about not needing it. He loved her acting as his nurse and he smiled at her.

When everyone left, Albert told Bethany something she wanted to hear. "Bethany, while that bear was mauling me, I was praying and asking God to forgive me. I accepted Jesus as my Savior. I was ready to anyway but just didn't get around to it. I want to thank you for pointing out my error in walking away from God. All it did was make me bitter and hateful. I kept telling myself I didn't believe in God but I knew better. I feel so peaceful now."

He stopped for a moment and noticed the smile on Bethany's face. He reached out and picked up her hand. "It wasn't God's fault that my folks were the way they were. When I get back, I shall go see them and apologize for not coming to see them more often. I can't apologize for not being a lawyer or a doctor, but I can for my behavior. I may even tell them I'm an engineer and very successful in my business. Thank you for your help in making me see the light," he exclaimed and squeezed her hand gently.

Bethany didn't pull her hand away. This was the man who saved her life. She had no doubt that she'd have died if Albert hadn't stepped in front of her. She felt that he was a brave man. All of the survivors treated her well and fussed over her cooking but there was something different about Albert's treatment.

The two had a nice visit while they waited for the group to return. Bethany asked questions about his occupation and what he did. Albert was pleased to tell her all about himself and his business. Bethany was a good listener to all the survivors.

Leslie and Jim headed up the hill while the other three headed west. Jim wanted to show her where all the food was located that they had seen on the trips to the top of the mountain.

While they were walking up the hill, Jim asked, "Do you really want to come to my mortuary and see what I do?" He thought perhaps she was only teasing but he wanted to make sure. If she did, he'd make a date for her to come and see his place of work. Not too many people asked to be invited to a mortuary.

"Yes, I do. And no, it wouldn't bother me in the least. I've seen a lot of distressful things in my journeys. It's all part of life. You seem pleased at your profession. Why do you like it?"

Jim wanted to word his reply just right and not offend his walking partner. "Leslie, I'm a Christian and Christians are supposed to talk to other people and tell them about how Jesus died on the cross for us. There are a lot of hurting people who come to the mortuary looking for answers. I can give that to them. I tell them that God doesn't make any mistakes even though we may think He does."

Jim stopped for a bit and looked at Leslie. He knew that Bethany was a Christian and that Leslie went along with things but he wasn't too sure about where she stood with his Christ. She had a strange look on her face but said nothing.

"Being a Christian is so easy. All you have to do is ask for forgiveness of sins and believe that Jesus died on the cross for your sins and accept Him as your Savior. Then if you really mean it, your life changes forever. And when problems come, you have a Savior to help you through them."

"You talk like Bethany. If there ever was a Christian that lived a good life, it is Bethany. She never gets mad, never swears, she just takes life as it is. I was a little upset at first with the crash because it was inconvenient but I knew that we'd find food to eat. That I learned in all my hiking expeditions. Bethany didn't know that but she just took the crash as something that happened and seemed to know that she'd be taken care of." Leslie looked at Jim as he was nodding his head.

Jim was pleased that Bethany was such a good example of a Christian. He was pleased that she was in the group of survivors. They all needed a Bethany to help them through this. Jim imagined himself being like Bethany as he knew God would take care of them but he sure didn't know how.

Leslie changed the subject. "Hey, look at those late berries. Oh, that's the good kind to eat. Let's pick those. And there are some of the dandelions still trying to grow. And I bet if we looked around we can find some roots."

Jim touched her shoulder. "What does that look like over there?"

"Bees!" she exclaimed.

The two hurried over to where they saw the big beehive. Sure enough they were honey bees. "How can we get the honey without getting stung," Leslie asked.

"Well, I suggest you take what we have and go down the hill a ways. Bee stings don't bother me but I think I can get some of the honey out without disturbing the bees. Just give me one of those containers so I have something to put the honey in." He took the container and then took a clean thin branch and made it in the shape of a ladle at the end. He slowly and carefully inserted it into the hive and brought out some honey. No bees objected. He repeated his steps several times until he had a good amount of honey in the container.

"Boy, I'm impressed," Leslie confessed. "I think you could do almost anything after seeing that. No bees even buzzed around you. I don't understand that."

"Well, it is a little cool today and they aren't flying around that much—just a few of the adventurous ones As long as we aren't too aggressive with them, they don't care. But if I whacked at the hive, you would see them coming after us and we wouldn't be able to outrun them," Jim explained.

"Oh, that honey is going to taste so good on some of Peter's pancakes. Shall we head back to camp and start cooking. This is so good."

"Leslie, think about what we were talking about earlier, will you?" Jim asked in a very soft voice. He wanted this young lady to understand salvation.

"I have been. I just need to understand it a little more," she answered.

"All you have to do is asked the Lord to help you understand and He will."

"That's what Bethany said. I may just try that. You and Eric and Bethany have something that I'd like to have. A peace or something I can't quite put my finger on. I've been watching you three. Don't worry, Jim. You've really impressed me to the point that I'm interested. I'm just not a person that jumps right into something without thinking it over," she explained.

"That's a good trait." He reached over and squeezed her hand and then took his hand away. He just wanted to let her know that he was pleased that she was thinking over everything that she had heard about Christianity since she landed on the island. He had every intention of talking with her again on that subject.

CHAPTER 23

The Airplane Pilot's Survey

When Jim and Leslie arrived in the camp, they were surprised to see that the other three hikers were already back. They were sitting around the camp fire visiting with each other.

"Just look what we found," Leslie bragged.

"Is that honey? Wow! I'm making some pancakes for lunch, Bethany. Is that okay?" Peter asked.

"That's fine with me. We'll just come into the airplane and watch you. Leslie and I can take a rest from cooking once in a while. What do you think about the honey, Albert?"

"Oh, that's going to be a great treat. I'm sure it's going to make my bear wounds feel much better."

The survivors entered the plane and just relaxed as they watched the master chef prepared their lunch. Then he not only prepared it but he served them all. Peter had to admit that he did like to cook but he sure made a lot more money as a newspaper reporter. It was a lot more nerve wracking of a job while cooking was an enjoyment. But he did like the money he made as a reporter. He considered himself a good newsman but he also knew that he was a good cook and he sure loved to cook.

"Now just what did you three men bring back in the way of food?" Leslie asked with her hands on her hips. She didn't see anything new around the camp.

"Oh, were we supposed to go food hunting? I thought this was just a little exercise trip," Dennis quipped.

"You know, I knew we were forgetting something," Peter remarked and grinned.

"Leslie, don't let them give you a bad time. We actually found another apple tree that still had a few apples on it and picked those. Peter found some real good roots to make his flour for the pancakes. We did bring back some things but we had some good exercise as well," Eric admitted.

Peter watched as everyone devoured the pancakes with the honey. Something different was always a treat. The honey could be used in a lot of different ways and where it came from, they should be able to go back and get some more. While no one complained about the food, they were always thankful for something special and honey was special. If they were home, no one would think it was anything extra. Being stranded on an island sure changed people's views on things and especially when it came to food items.

When they were through eating, they all decided to go back outside and make a fire. There wasn't a lot to be done now. They could all relax. But they heard a strange noise and looked around. It didn't sound like an animal. Eric didn't think it sounded like a bear but there was a slight resemblance in the sound.

"Everyone, please be quiet for a minute," Eric instructed.

The sound grew louder and louder and then they knew what it was. It was an airplane coming right over their island. They watched speechless as the plane drew nearer. Eric looked at the stunned faces of the survivors. They didn't know if it was real or something they were all hoping for and imagined.

Peter watched with the others as the plane dropped a huge box not too far from their camp. The airplane buzzed around them a couple of times and they all waved. It appeared that the pilot of the plane was looking over everything so he could report it to his superiors. It seemed that he was counting the people standing on the island waving at him.

He was looking over their condition. Well, he'd have nothing but good things to report back to whomever he reported to.

When the plane took off, they ran to the box and Dennis tried to open it.

"We'll have to get that crow bar that we found. It's not going to open that easy. It's a wonder it didn't break open when it hit the ground. It has to be built out of a strong type of wood to endure a drop like that," Peter exclaimed.

Eric ran into the luggage area where they had stored the tools and brought the crow bar to Dennis. He was amazed how excited Dennis was to open the box. They all were but you'd think this was Christmas and they were opening Christmas presents. It was always nice when something different came along in their adventure.

Finally, the wood gave way and the box opened. There was a letter in the box right on the top so they'd be sure to spot it and not let it get lost in all the other things in the huge box. Eric took the letter and read it to them.

"To the survivors of Flight 509: We have included some food in the box as we are sure you're probably at the point of starvation." When he read that, everyone had a good laugh.

"If they only knew how much we had to eat, thanks to Leslie and Bethany. Oh, yes thanks to Chef Peter too," Dennis grinned.

Eric continued reading. "It will likely be two or three weeks before we can make a rescue attempt. One reason is that there is no place on the island to land an airplane. Another thing is that the water is too shallow to bring in a ship. The military is preparing to sail a ship out in the ocean quite some ways away from the island and then smaller boats will come after you. But we have to have time to make all the arrangements and time for the ship to sail there. We also have to have permission from the government in Washington before we can do anything."

"Now, we could be here all winter waiting for permission from the government," Jim laughed. He'd never seen Washington act on anything very quickly. It would seem that this rescue would be one thing that the president could just say, go rescue them immediately but he wasn't sure that was how it would work.

"Well, look at this food, will you? Health bars! I may never eat another one after getting off this island. I know they have been filling and healthy but enough is enough. Why couldn't they have sent some beans, rice or some other stables? At least we have more juice. Hey they even sent some candy bars. Jim you read the label on the ones you take," Peter ordered.

"Yeah, you can count on that," Jim answered.

"Don't count those health bars out," Bethany stated. "I can take them and grind them up with some berries and other things and make the best cake you ever ate," she informed them.

"Really?" Eric asked.

"Yes, I know we're all a little tired of those bars so Leslie, Peter and I will make something else out of them. We can even make a casserole putting in bear meat and greens along with the wild onions. With us having an oven to cook in changes everything. Don't you worry we'll fix them up so you won't even know that you're eating health bars." Bethany smiled as everyone looked relieved. The health bars were good but anything gets tiring after eating them for quite some time.

"Look at these two way radios. They will probably connect with the ship when it arrives but in the meantime we can play with them. Well, let's see what else is in the box and then we shall try out these things," Eric suggested.

"Is your Spanish speaking any better now?" teased Dennis. "That's probably who we would talk to if we used the radios."

"Oh, let's hope that's not what we get on those two-way radios. But you know that we need to thank those people who contacted the United States officials for us," Peter stated. "They really were our rescuers. We should get the best thank you card we can find and send it to Spain. But how would we know where and to whom to send it?"

"We can always find out who received the message and see if we can pinpoint the actual place," suggested Eric. "I'm sure whoever he contacted most likely took his name and phone number. We'll be sure to check into that when we get back home."

In the box were some more blankets. They probably didn't know that there were plenty of them on the airplane. They also found some different mixes—stove top stuffing, salad dressing, taco shells and dressing. Well, at least those things looked good. The herb dressing that Peter and Bethany made wasn't all that bad, but a change would be nice, Eric believed.

After the box was emptied, they all helped carry the supplies into the airplane. Bethany and Leslie directed them just where they could store everything. They had things just as they wanted it and they could instantly find what they needed for cooking. They certainly didn't want the men to put the new groceries just anywhere. They already had a place for spices they informed the men.

The two ladies had insisted that the bear rug be placed in front of the steps so they didn't carry any dirt into their "house." The men did exactly as the ladies asked. They had found a whisk brush and kept the floor cleaned along with keeping everything in order. Bethany and Leslie rather enjoyed keeping the airplane clean and the groceries and other things in a proper place.

Eric just smiled at them. Now that there wasn't that much work to do, the two ladies were making work. But it was nice to go into the airplane and have everything looking nice and clean and in order.

With not a whole lot of work to do, Peter usually helped the ladies with the cooking. They were pleased as he always suggested different things they could eat and showed them different ways of cooking the meats. He thought it was about time that someone caught another salmon.

"Jim, didn't you complain that you wanted to fish for a salmon?" Peter asked.

"Yeah, I do. You want one for dinner tonight?" he asked.

"We sure do. This time we are going to bake it with all different types of herbs. No more frying."

Dennis provided Jim with the fishing equipment. He'd have liked to have done the fishing but Jim was so anxious to give it a try. Jim had fished a lot at home and was no beginner.

He let Dennis put the worm on the hook as he seemed to want to so much. Then Jim took the fishing pole to the edge of the water and threw the line out into the water as far as he could. It had been out there for five minutes and nothing happened.

He reeled the line back in. "How come I didn't catch a fish?" he asked Dennis.

"Because you didn't move the line around, that's why. This time throw out the line and keep moving it," Dennis suggested.

Jim did as he was told and in less than a minute he was reeling in a big salmon. He was pleased. He had missed fishing and reeling in that big salmon was a thrill.

CHAPTER 24

Jim's Talk with Leslie

When the excitement died down concerning the box, Eric changed the subject. He had been out looking over the items in the luggage compartment and knew that they were getting very low on wood. They needed to fill the empty space in the luggage compartment with wood just in case snow came before they were rescued.

"We don't have much wood left. Do I have any volunteer to take that axe we found and chop up some more wood?" Eric asked.

"Peter and I will get the wood," Albert volunteered.

"Thanks," Eric said.

"We're also getting low on wild onions and they add so much to my food. Do we dare go back to the first place and get some?" Bethany asked Eric. She knew he didn't want them going back there, but the wild onions just added great flavor to the soups, stews, casseroles and other dishes. She even put them on the bear steaks and that brought out a good flavor.

"Has anyone seen any wild onions anywhere else?" Eric asked looking at Jim and Dennis. They had said there were all kinds of things growing just a little ways up the hill. So they'd be the logical one to find them.

"Yes, there's a patch not too far. If you wish, I'll go get enough to last us a month. You can count on us being here that long if Washington has to approve of our rescue," Jim stated firmly.

"That seems so strange to me. If I were in charge, I'd send someone immediately to rescue the survivors of an airplane crash. I don't understand why it would take so long to make a decision." Bethany commented.

"I wish you were in charge, Bethany. But we're in international waters as far as we know. However, we could be on some island that belongs to a specific country and then they'd have to have permission to rescue us. It all gets complicated. It will probably be the navy that will do the rescuing since they can't land a plane. That will take some time to get here. But friends, we aren't starving, we're with good people, and we have a good roof over our heads. What more can we ask?" Jim asked.

"Only to go back home," Dennis answered and smiled. "You know when we do return to our homes, I'm sure going to miss every one of you. It will not be the same after all we've been through together. All of you are very special to me."

"Now, let's not get sentimental or you'll have us all bawling," Albert quipped.

"Yeah," everyone said. But they knew they'd miss one another.

"We can't just part like that. Didn't you say that we're all from Pittsburg? Why can't we set up meetings twice a year and meet and go out to eat together and check on each other's lives? I don't want to lose track of any of you," Bethany remarked.

"Me either," Leslie agreed.

"Yes, we shall do that. We'll find what days are best for most of us and what time of year and we shall meet again. I feel like you're all my family," Eric declared. "Now that the sentimental time is over, please go get Bethany some wild onions!"

Jim smiled. He had been so wrapped up in the sentiment that he forgot he had an assignment.

"Dennis, I need you for a project. Leslie, why don't you go with Jim and then you'll know where the wild onions are just in case we need more. Take a couple of bags and bring them back full," Eric suggested.

"Sure," Leslie agreed and picked up a shovel. Jim had some bags to carry their findings and offered to trade, but Leslie kept the shove. She wasn't an invalid. She could carry a shovel, she informed him.

Jim just laughed. He rather liked an independent gal and Leslie was definitely independent.

She always enjoyed going with Jim as she learned a lot from him and he was very entertaining. He could tell some stories that would make you shiver or some that would make you laugh.

They took their time as they walked up the hill. There weren't a lot of duties now and they certainly didn't need to be in a hurry. Jim told her all about his and Dennis' trips to the top of the mountain and the different things they saw when they were up there. It did seem as though it would be fun to walk to the top, she thought.

"Peter likes these big roots of this particular plant. I don't even know what type a plant it is but he said they were like a potato and they made good flour. We should dig some of these and make him happy by bringing some back to him. It doesn't take much to make Peter happy when it comes to cooking," Leslie remarked.

"Yes, that will make Peter happy. I really think he likes to cook. He sure seems happy when he's cooking but he's careful not to interfere with Bethany's cooking. I don't think he wants to hurt her feelings," Jim answered. He smiled at Leslie. He enjoyed being with this young woman. He had prayed for her.

"Leslie, whenever I think about what it could have been like here, I'm just amazed. We haven't suffered at all, with the exception of Bethany's fall, Albert's bear wrestling, and my allergy attack. But each of us healed up with no bad affects left. Even the scars on Albert's face are gone. I don't know about his arms. I think that God has been so good to us by supplying all this food and our new home in the airplane. It's like a small studio apartment. Only we made two rooms out of it."

"I know. When we sit around the wood stove and visit or listen to your harmonica playing, it's just like we were at home visiting with friends. There's no panic because we aren't home. No one complains about the food with the exception of the overload of health bars. This is terrible to say, but I don't mind spending another month here while Washington gives their approval for our rescue," Leslie stated.

"I know. It's so different from being home and having to go to work every day. It's like a vacation."

"It sure is," she agreed.

Then Jim became real serious. "Have you thought any more about what we talked about before—about God and His Son Jesus?" He had made the remarked very slowly and sincerely. He didn't want to offend her but she had promised to think about what he and Bethany had told her about Christ.

"Yes I have and I did what you said I should. I asked for forgiveness and asked Him to be my Savior. I felt a great sense of peace—the peace I saw on Bethany's face. I do believe in Jesus and I do believe that He died on the cross for me."

Jim was so excited that that he hugged her. Then he back off. "I'm sorry, but you just made my day. I've been praying for you that you would understand salvation. I'm so pleased that you're now a Christian."

"You don't need to be sorry that you hugged me, Jim. I've been waiting for a hug from you for a long time," Leslie confessed.

"Really?" Jim asked and gave her another hug. Then he took her in his arms and kissed her and Leslie returned the kiss.

"I'm not quite sure what just happened," Jim stated.

"Oh, it didn't just happen," Leslie remarked smiling. "It's been going on for a while. I saw how you looked at me from time to time and wondered if you were ever going to tell me your feelings. But I have an idea we should wait until we're home or at least on the way home before we say anything to anyone."

"You're right. Are you still going to wait for three years before you settle down and get married?" Jim asked with a smile hoping she answered what he was wishing for and hoping for.

"Not if a certain man asks me to marry him sooner," she answered.

"Marry me, Leslie, you beautiful woman." Jim looked at her. He was a happy man. He didn't think he had a chance with this wilderness hiker. He knew he loved her from the beginning but he wouldn't get involved with a woman who wasn't a Christian. Now that she was, he was one pleased man.

Leslie hugged him and answered, "Yes, I'll marry you."

"We better get back to the camp before they come looking for us," Jim stated.

"Well, perhaps we better dig the onions before we go back empty handed. They'll wonder what we're up to if we come back with nothing."

"Oh, yes you're right. We'll dig them and get some of those roots that Peters likes to cook with. I can just imagine what the group would say if we came into camp without anything."

The two went to work and soon had their bags full of onions and roots. They threw in a few apples along the way and leisurely walked down the trail.

"Hey, you two, you've been gone long enough to plant and grow those onions," Dennis stated. "What took you so long?

"We didn't know there was any hurry so we took our time and looked around the country for a little while. There sure is plenty of food in that area. We could probably live all winter just collecting roots, berries, fruit from there," Jim commented and held up his bag.

"You didn't see any more bears or deer or any other kind of animal around that area?" asked Dennis.

"There are plenty of rabbits running around everywhere. You almost step on them. They don't seem to be too afraid of us. And they are good to eat the way Peter and Bethany cooks them," Leslie answered.

"I have no problem having roast rabbit, rabbit enchiladas, rabbit stew or anything else that Bethany dreams up to make out of the little creatures. But one thing I know is that we better start finishing that bear before it goes bad," Eric stated.

"There isn't anything left on it to eat. Bethany and Leslie dried the meat that was left. They didn't want it to spoiled," Peter remarked. "I think Bethany and I will make a big dish of something tonight with the dried bear meat and then we'll likely have only a meal or two left. What you see on that bear is bone and I haven't been able to think of how to cook the bone so we can eat it," Peter informed them and smiled at Bethany.

"Oh, give the bones to Bethany. She can make food out of anything, I do believe," Dennis remarked.

"I think you over rate my ability. About all the bones are good for is to flavor the stew or soup. Now if we got desperate, we could grind them up and they would be a good source of calcium for us. But they have been there too long. I think someone should take the carcass down and get rid of it," she stated.

"See, I told you she could make food out of anything," Dennis quipped.

CHAPTER 25

Peter's Pictures

One evening they all decided to view the pictures that Peter had taken. He set the camera on the table and let it run in slide mode and they all sat back and watched. It was a good thing he had a pretty good size screen on his camera.

"When did you take these pictures? Look, there's Bethany cooking the bear meat and there is the skinned bear hanging in the tree. And there is the bear rug we walk on before we go into the airplane. Here comes Leslie and Bethany with food. Oh, there's Eric with the crowbar and Dennis opening the box," Albert remarked.

"Oh, you even took a picture of me with all my bandages," Albert remarked. "I sure didn't look too good. I didn't realize I looked so bad. No wonder everyone was giving me a little sympathy."

There were so many different pictures that they felt as though they were at the movies watching a picture. There were some comical pictures taken and that's when everyone heard the victim objecting. "Don't put that in your book. Just because I happened to fall down doesn't mean I'm clumsy and that's what people will think about me," Dennis declared.

"If you put that one of me stumbling up the stairs to the airplane, I'm coming after you," Eric promised.

There was a picture of Jim and Dennis dragging the deer into camp. Everyone had been so busy watching the two men with their prize deer that they hadn't noticed Peter shooting pictures.

He shot pictures of Albert working on the engine of the airplane. Everyone was surprised that there were so many pictures. Only Leslie had caught him capturing the moments on his camera. He seemed to take a picture of all the important things that had happened to them. There were funny ones and some good ones. Dennis didn't care too much for the pictures of the skeletons. They saw the big grave and almost wished that hadn't been included but it was part of their story.

"After we get home, how long will it take you to write the book?" Dennis asked.

"Well, I have most of it all ready written, I just have to type it up. Everyday I put down that day's events. Some of the things I wrote, I won't use and others I will. I have a picture of Albert when he was unconscious. Can I use that?"

"Why not? No one else here wrestled a bear. I suppose you have to add that Eric and you killed it when I couldn't. Well, they need some credit," Albert agreed.

Finally Peter ran out of pictures.

"That was really good, Peter. I'm sure the rest of us had digital cameras in our carry-on bags but we didn't think to use them. This sure has been a nice evening and an evening of remembering. I wish we could all have pictures of everything that you took," Bethany remarked.

"Once the book is published, I shall send you all copies. We all need something to remind us about the great time we had here. It's been quite a vacation. One I shall never forget," Peter exclaimed.

"I don't plan on forgetting our good times and the fellowship we had with one another," declared Leslie.

"Now, first thing in the morning, I want us all to stand by the airplane and have a group picture taken. I want someone to write Flight 509 on the airplane and we'll stand just below that. Don't let me forget. We'll take several shots to ensure that we do get at least one good one of all of you. And I don't want any horns over anyone's head, Dennis," Peter exclaimed sternly and looked right at Dennis.

"Me, give someone horns? You have me mixed up with Albert," Dennis quipped and roared with laughter.

Jim played his harmonica again and the group sang some of the hymns and then headed for bed.

Quite early in the morning as they were having their breakfast, they heard a plane headed their way. Everyone quickly finished the breakfast, stepped out of the airplane, went out in the open area and watched the airplane as it circled their area. It looked as if they were dropping another box. That could only mean that they weren't going to be rescued anytime too soon—at least not today.

"Well, there'll probably be some more health bars as that's just what we need," Dennis quipped and grinned. Although when he thought of the dessert and the casserole that Bethany made out of the last bunch, he decided he shouldn't say anything.

"Get your crowbar, Dennis, and open the box," Eric suggested. It seemed that Dennis really enjoyed opening the boxes so Eric let him have the job.

Dennis grabbed the crowbar and hurried back to the box. Once he had it opened there on top was another note. He handed it to Eric.

"Greetings Survivors, this is to inform you that you'll be rescued in one week from today. Please have everything ready that you wish to take with you. Since you appeared to be very healthy from the other pilot's viewing, we decided to send you some different types of food. He said you had a stovepipe coming out of the roof of the airplane. It doesn't sound plausible but we took his word for it. So we have sent you some quick and easy meals where you just add water and bake or cook on top of the stove. You probably haven't had any milk so you won't be too opposed to powered milk or canned milk. We shall see you in one week."

Eric was pleased with the contents of the box. They all looked through the food and found some cans of ham and other meats. That was nice since their bear meat was long gone. There were boxes of noodles and spaghetti and many other types of food they hadn't had for some time. They decided that they wouldn't worry too much about gathering food as they would probably not eat all that was in the box.

It would be a week of leisure. Eric figured that it probably wouldn't be as interesting to everyone as when they had to work and accomplish something. But they all had worked hard and a week of fun wouldn't be bad. They had occasionally gone for a swim in the ocean when it was warm enough and they would likely do that a few more times if the weather gave them a nice sunny day. Eric wasn't quite sure that with nothing to do was going to be good for them. Perhaps he should find some type of game to play or something to keep them busy.

"Peter, we're supposed to remind you to take a picture of us by the airplane. I'll write 509 on the airplane and then you take several pictures. You know that to get a good one of Albert and Jim is going to be hard," Dennis remarked quite seriously.

"Speak for yourself," Albert quipped.

They lined up in front of the airplane and tried to behave but some of the pictures had horns on some of the people. They quietly put horns on Bethany and Leslie without them knowing it. Peter had a remote clicker and he was able to be in the picture. So he didn't notice the horns. But the comics did leave several pictures without any horns so that there would be good ones for the book. There weren't too many pictures that Peter was included in since he was the camera man.

The survivors enjoyed the picture taking. They insisted on taking some of Peter and made him stand by the wrecked shelter. Then they had him stand in the middle of the two ladies. They took several of the group each one taking a turn at the camera. They insisted that Peter had to be in several of the pictures. He did what they asked him to do knowing that he was the one that would choose the pictures for the book.

Eric noticed that it took quite a while to put the contents of the second box away. He checked on the wood and noted that there was plenty in the luggage department. They made sure there was enough to last through the winter but he was sure glad they weren't going to have to use it. These months of summer had been all right but if snow came, well that would be a different story. He could just imagine that the survivors would get a little annoyed at being enclosed in such a small space if they had to spend the winter there and weren't able to go out in the cold for very long.

The group scattered after the pictures were taken. Eric noticed and he and Bethany were the only ones in camp now. One of the new rules was that two had to be in camp so Eric stayed with Bethany. No one should be anywhere alone since they knew there were bears on the island. Bethany was working on dinner. Even though the others didn't have work to do they wanted to get their exercise and wandered off into the woods.

Eric slowly walked over to Bethany and sat down on one of the couches made from the chairs.

"Bethany, what are you going to do when this is all over? Will you be going back to your aunt's house when you get home?"

"Yes, they encouraged me to come live with them," she answered.

"Would it be all right if I came over sometime and took you out to dinner? I'd like to see you now and then," Eric said not too sure that he put it the way he wanted to. He watched Bethany's face and was puzzled.

"Eric, I'm all ready spoken for. It wouldn't be right for me to date someone else, but I want to thank you for asking me. If I were free I'd be glad to go out with you but you see, I'm already engaged. However, I'd be pleased for you to come and visit with me and my aunt. You have been so great to take care of me on the airplane when it crashed. You have been a very thoughtful person. I admire you greatly."

Eric was shocked. He didn't want to be admired. He wanted her to love him. "You don't have a ring," he stated slowly.

"No, but I will have shortly after I get home. But thank you for thinking of me. All you men have been like big brothers to me. You really mean a lot to me and I'm going to miss you," Bethany explained. She hated to see the hurt in Eric's eyes. There were times that she knew he was watching her and she was worried that he was getting a little too interested and she didn't know what to do about it. She didn't know what to say to ease the hurt look on his face.

"Well, whoever your fiancé is, he's one lucky man," Eric exclaimed and slowly walked out of the airplane. He never would have guessed that she had someone at home waiting for her. She never talked about him, never seemed concerned about someone she wasn't able to see. If he was engaged and stuck on an island, he sure would be trying to get back or trying to get word to them. But they did do all they could. He was so disappointed. Bethany was the first young woman that he had ever felt that he would like to marry. Well maybe the second one as he thought about Lisa. "I hope whoever he is appreciates her," he growled to himself.

Then Eric thought some more about the girl he had dated a few times. He knew that she was interested in getting married, but something always held him back. He just wasn't ready. But since Bethany was already taken, maybe he'd pursue a relationship with Lisa. She was a beautiful girl and she had a sweet and loving spirit. Lisa was a good Christian girl. He knew it would take some time to get over Bethany's rejection. He felt that he loved Bethany the first day he met her on the airplane.

The next day when Bethany and Peter were fixing lunch for the hikers, he asked her if she had any definite plans when she got home. "I'd like to go over to your aunt's house and visit with you now and then once we get home. You've been a great help to us and you're a great gal. I've never had much to do with religion, but after watching you, I think there's something to it. You have more patience than anyone I ever knew and you live your life as I always thought a Christian should."

"Now that's the best compliment you could give me. You know Leslie wasn't a Christian when she first landed here but she is now. Albert wasn't either but he is now. You're our one holdout. You know it's so easy to become a Christian and you would live a life that's so much more peaceful than you ever had before."

"I know, I have thought about it. But I was brought up so different. But, Bethany, I'm thinking about it," he said and smiled at her. He knew right then there was no use of asking her to go out with him because he had an idea that she'd only date a Christian man and he knew that it wasn't right for him to become a Christian just so he could date the beautiful girl.

"Now, you aren't going to cook these packaged goods just like they are? You're going to put some of your special spices and things in them aren't you? We've all been used to Bethany's cooking and this manufactured stuff just isn't going to be the same as your dishes," Peter stated.

Bethany laughed so hard and Peter joined her. "I'm going to spice it up just for you, Peter. But you know every bit as much as I do about cooking so you can help me spice it up. I'm hoping we can have one more rabbit stew though. What do you think?"

"Oh, we have to have one more rabbit stew and at least a salmon or two before we leave our island. We should have that on the last day. I have to admit though, that ham we had yesterday wasn't too bad. Those canned ravioli dishes sure needed your touch. You know we should plan a great big dinner for the last day and then have a good breakfast the morning they plan to rescue us. It would be a celebration breakfast."

"You're right, Peter. We shall plan that. Like one of our celebration times we've had since we've been here. This is really going to be a celebration. I sure hope we can all meet often and talk about our times here. I'm going to miss all of you. It makes me a little sad to think we're going to be away from each other."

"Me too," he answered.

Lunch was ready and the hikers were back. Everyone was enjoying a different type of lunch. They all talked about what would happen when they returned home. Things would be different they were sure.

"I don't want to get back into the same old rat race," Peter stated. "You won't believe this, but I may just go back to being a chef and open my own restaurant. That would be after I write my book and put this plane crash story on the front page of every newspaper in the nation."

"We're going to watch for that newspaper," Leslie remarked. "I want one to put up and save. I know it's going to be a good article."

"You really think you want to go back to cooking. Isn't that a stressful job?" Dennis asked.

"Not near as stressful as being a reporter. I could never shove a mike in someone's face that had lost a loved one and try to make them tell how they felt. That was what I didn't like about being a reporter. But as for the restaurant, if Bethany came to work for me, we could really put out some meals. We'd have the best restaurant in town. I know five people who would visit us often."

Bethany only smiled.

"I'd be one of the first to visit the restaurant," Albert exclaimed.

"I'd be the second," Dennis said. "Bethany, why don't you just marry me and take care of me? I could eat your cooking the rest of my life. You're one good cook. We could always invite the rest of the islanders over often to eat your cooking."

"I think there is more to marriage than being a cook, Dennis. You can hire a good cook anywhere. But I'll keep that in mind," Bethany remarked while shaking her head and smiling. If Dennis couldn't joke around, he wouldn't know what to say.

"People, we only have two more days. Has everyone pretty well decided on what they are taking with them?" Eric asked.

"Yes," Leslie and Bethany echoed.

"I think we all are pretty well packed," Jim answered.

"Well, let's make sure we have everything together. We don't want them coming and we have to run around and gathering up things. I know there are some souvenirs that we all have found that we want to take. Albert, are you taking the bear rug?"

"No! I don't want that bear rug around to remind of that horrifying event. If there is someone who wants it, they can have the thing," he exclaimed and shivered.

"Anyone want it?" Eric asked.

Leslie waited and when no one answered she said, "I'd love to have it if no one else is interested. It's really rather neat. It would look real nice in my living room. I'd remember this island and my friends every time I saw it."

"It is neat," Jim remarked. "I think Leslie should have it since she really wants it and no one else seems interested."

"Okay that's settled. It will probably be late in the afternoon when they come this Monday, but we'll be ready no matter what time they arrive," Eric suggested.

There wasn't much to do so Peter and Eric decided to go for a walk together. When they were quite a ways away from camp, Peter questioned the man. "Say, Eric, you've looked a little down in the dumps lately. Is there something wrong? Now you should be happy that we're going home. What's wrong?"

"From day one, Peter, I've had a crush on Bethany. She sat with me on the airplane. I helped her while we were sailing the skies. This was her first flight and she was a little nervous. I helped her when the plane crashed. She was so pale and didn't quite know what to do. I fell in love with her then but I didn't think anyone should partner up while we were on the island. I could see how it might cause problems so I never said anything to her. Then yesterday, I asked if I could come see her and take her out once we returned home."

"What did she say?"

"You won't believe what she said. She told she couldn't go out with me because she was engaged. I couldn't believe it. She didn't appear to be anxious to get home because a fiancé was waiting for her. She seemed perfectly content in doing what she was doing here. If I felt bad, can you imagine how Albert is going to take this?" Eric asked.

"Oh, yes. Albert fell for her right at the first. But Bethany must have told him. She wouldn't lead him on deliberately. But he's sure taking it better than you or I. I tried to get her to date me but she turned the conversation over to religion and I knew right then she wouldn't date someone who wasn't a Christian. She never mentioned being engaged or having someone at home waiting for her."

"I'm sure that Bethany knows how Albert feels. But I wonder if he really believes that she has a fiancé waiting for her. It seems that sometimes it's hard to get something through to Albert. I hope we don't have an explosion over all this when it finally sinks in," Eric stated.

"I guess we just have to wait and see. Did you hear that silly proposal that Dennis gave to her? Leave it to Dennis. Now the only one that isn't in love with Bethany is Jim and that surprises me. They are both so easy going that they'd make a good couple. He treats her like a princess but I never see him watching her. It's like he considers her a sister or a relative. Now if she just wasn't so beautiful... But she is."

The two walked on a ways and finally returned to the camp. It did Eric good to talk things over with Peter. He felt a little better. If Peter noticed that he was down in the dumps he better straighten up right now before everyone in camp tries to console him. He always had a hard time hiding his feelings.

Peter thought about what Eric had said. So Bethany was engaged and just didn't tell anyone about it. He was quite sure that she had told Albert. Albert was very protective of Bethany but he didn't just hang around with her. Peter knew he liked her being his nurse when he was hurt. Bethany had to somehow give him the information about her engagement in a way that he accepted it.

If things were different, he would marry Bethany in a minute. But he wasn't good enough for her and he knew it and Bethany was already engaged. That was some fortunate man that she was going to marry. Then he wondered just how much truth was in Dennis' proposal. Was it all in fun or was he serious. Peter had seen him watching Bethany from time to time. If Dennis ever proposed to a girl, it would probably be just like the way he proposed to Bethany.

But Peter had to admit that Dennis was a lot of fun. He and Jim sure formed a bond between them. Walking up that big mountain twice had caused a close friendship. He was friends with everyone but he sure wished he had a close friendship with that beautiful young lady!

Peter began to think about when they would be rescued. He sure was going to miss this whole group. He'd probably miss Albert more than any of the rest of them. He had learned to respect the man.

CHAPTER 26

The Last Sunday

It was Sunday morning and the survivors decided that they would have a good Sunday service right after breakfast. When they finished eating, Jim took out his harmonica and they began singing some hymns. By now Peter had learned most of them and he was singing at the top of his lungs along with the rest of the group. He loved to sing and he didn't care what he was singing. But the hymns they sang always told a story and he often thought about them after the singing was finished.

"He's interested in Christianity even if he won't admit it," thought Eric. "He just won't make a commitment. Perhaps when he gets back home he'll think more about the Bible and our Savior." He could see an interest in Peter that he'd never seen before. He would pray a little harder for the man.

They had a fire going and it was nice and cozy in the airplane. They sang a lot longer than they usually did as this would be their last Sunday service. In the middle of their song service there came a loud pounding on the door. Everyone stopped. Who could possibly be outside?

Eric slowly opened the door. "Come in," he said to the navy man. "You're a day early."

"Yes I am, but I'm rather glad to be here. You're having a church service," he stated in a surprised voice as he stepped inside. He looked around. "My word, look at this airplane. It looks like a hotel room. I can't believe this. Where ever did you find that stove? This is amazing. For a while we felt so sorry for you being stranded for so many months but I see now you all just had one big vacation."

"Well, we just made the most out of everything we found," Eric remarked.

"Oh, I can see that. Well, I hope I haven't spoiled anything coming early. By the way, my name is Nathan Billows. Now before we start moving everything to the boat, I'm supposed to see where you buried the ones who didn't survive. Would you mind showing me?"

"Sure, some of the rest of the group may want to go with us," Eric remarked and looked around. All heads nodded except Dennis. Someone had to watch the camp and he'd volunteer.

"Now let me introduce you to this group," Eric suggested. "This is Bethany McMillan, this is Leslie Morris, Peter Jameson, Albert Desmond, Dennis Williams, Jim Majors, and I'm Eric Johnson."

"I'm pleased to meet all of you. You're a great group of survivors. Now let's go to that grave site," Nathan suggested.

"We always leave someone to watch the camp," Dennis informed the man. "I'll volunteer to do that." It was a little too close to those skeletons and he wasn't about to visit them again.

The group walked over to the huge grave that held those who didn't survive the crash. Nathan looked at the makeshift grave. "How did you manage to get the people off the airplane and into this grave? What did you dig it with?"

"We dropped them in the water and let the bodies float down. There was a big hole right there and we used that. Then we covered them with everything we could find. We knew that since we weren't rescued the first day, it could be a while. And we knew there were things in the plane that we could make use of so we had to move the bodies," Eric explained.

"That plane didn't just land right where it is? How did you get the plane in just the right place?" Nathan asked.

"Peter and Albert fixed one of the engines so it could be driven just a little ways up on the beach. They worked for over three weeks and finally got it running."

"Now where did the stove come from?" was Nathan's next question.

"Let's walk a little ways further and I'll show you." Eric did everything he could to hold a straight face. He wondered what Nathan would say when he saw the skeletons sitting up as if they were having a conversation.

"This land looks as though it might have been cultivated at one time," Nathan declared.

"That's what we thought. Then we found these two gentlemen," Eric stated and pointed to the skeletons.

"Whoa." Nathan backed up a bit and stared at the remains of two people. This was so weird. Was this group trying to play a joke on him? He looked at his companions and they were all smiling.

"It looks just like they are having tea and talking, doesn't it," Jim commented.

"It looks a little too much like that. Did one of you arrange these skeletons in this position?" he asked slowly. He couldn't imagine someone touching the skeletons to move them in that position. He shivered.

"No, we didn't," Jim answered. "But there are people who believe that after someone dies they should stay in a seated position whether they're in the ground or on top of it. So that's what we figured happened to these two people. We looked for a third survivor but never found one. He may have somehow left the island."

Jim noticed that the man didn't go too close to the skeletons. But Jim took another closer look. He just couldn't figure out what they might have died from. He sure would like to know. He didn't think it was quite right for them to move the skeletons with the bodies of those who didn't survive. But he sure wished someone would run a test to see if they could find out the cause of death.

"Is this where you found the stove?" Nathan asked still keeping his distance from the two skeletons.

"Just a little further over there is the spot where the stove was. We just couldn't believe it when we saw it. But we knew it would be easier to cook on that than over a fire so we brought it back to camp,"

Albert admitted. "And then when it got cooler, it sure warmed up the airplane."

"Well, let's get back to our camp and let me ask the other questions that I need to know." Nathan was glad to get away from the skeletons. It was a creepy scene and it looked as if they were staring right at him because he invaded their space. Well he would get right out of their presence.

Everyone entered the airplane and sat down. "Now what did you do with the luggage?" the navy man asked.

"What we could use, we used. Everyone took their own. We saved the rest of it and stored it in the luggage department. But we felt free to use what we could to survive. We found tools, food, clothes and all sorts of things we needed for survival. We knew that the ones that didn't survive had no use for them." Eric looked at Nathan. He had asked that question as if… Well, he didn't like the way the man ask about the luggage. It's as though he thought they shouldn't have opened anyone else's luggage.

"I see. I guess that was necessary all right. Now if you have your things, you can start moving them out to the boat. I have a small boat that I brought on shore. I can take two people at a time and some luggage. I'll take you out to the smaller ship which is pretty good size and then we'll meet the big ship further out in the ocean."

Nathan looked at Jim. "Don't I know you, sir?" he asked.

"Yes, you do. I was at your wife's funeral two years ago," Jim answered.

"Yes, you were the mortician weren't you?" Nathan asked.

Jim nodded in agreement.

Everyone stared at Jim and laughed. "So that's what you do for a living. Now I know why you didn't want to tell any of us what your occupation was. All this time I've been a buddy to an undertaker? No wonder you were interested in those skeletons," Dennis remarked and visibly shivered.

"Well that ended one nice friendship," Jim laughed.

"No, not exactly. I know you now, but believe me if I'd known you were a mortician I probably wouldn't have become so friendly. Well, I'll be…" Dennis couldn't get over the fact that Jim worked in a mortuary.

He just shook his head and stared at him. If he was a mortician, he wouldn't tell anyone either. But that was one thing he would never be.

"Jim, are you interested in coming back and helping bring the bodies back so their relatives can claim them," Nathan asked.

"If I'm needed, I will but if you have plenty of others, I'd rather not because I have some plans when I first get home. So, let's wait and see. You may have plenty of help along that line without me." Jim definitely had plans and he didn't want something as unpleasant as this to interfere.

"Now, I want to tell you that there's a reporter on the main ship. He wanted to come with me, but I wouldn't let him. I knew he'd interfere with what I needed to do. He's one of those reporters who twist everything you say. Be very careful how you word things when you talk with him," Nathan warned.

"Nathan, I'm a newspaper reporter and I plan on writing the story. Actually, I have it all written but I just need to type it and send it off to my editor. I have pictures and everything that I plan on having a big front page story. Perhaps you can run interference between my friends and this other reporter. I'd like the story to be factual and not someone's fantasy." Peter looked at Nathan and the man was nodding his head in agreement.

"I didn't want to bring the man on this trip but I was forced into it. They said they had to have some reporter to tell the story. Since you're a reporter, I'll do my best to keep him quiet but it won't be easy. If anyone of you answers one of his questions he'll keep on bugging you for more answers. But you should tell him that you have already talked with Peter so you'll not be answering his questions. If you stick to that, you probably can avoid him, but no promises."

Eric spoke up. "I suggest that we make one person the spokesman and when he asks us questions, we can tell him who the spokes person is and that's the only one of the survivors who will talk with him."

"Hey, that's a good idea. I suggest we let Albert be the spokesperson. From what he has told me, he's had to handle them before and he knows how to do it," Peter suggested. "Besides, with Albert's height and build, he can be very intimidating. I wouldn't pick a fight with a man like that."

CHAPTER 27

The Captain and the Reporter

Nathan suggested that they take the two ladies over to the smaller ship first. If they would bring their suitcases and belongings, he'd start moving everyone every one to the ship.

"Is that where the reporter is?" asked Albert.

"No, I wouldn't even let him come this far. He's on the main ship," Nathan answered.

"That's good because I don't want the girls to be there with the reporter without one of us with them for protection. I've had a few run-ins with reporters and if you get a certain type, they'll drag information out of you," Albert exclaimed.

"I understand," Nathan said as he and the men carried the ladies' suitcases and other supplies to the small boat.

"Bethany, are you going to leave all that dried food here?" Eric asked.

"Yes, someone else may get stranded and that dried food will last a long time. The next group won't have such a hard time as we did at first. It would almost be nice to come back some day and spend a week or two here," Bethany remarked. "We'd have the food we needed already waiting for us."

"Hey, wouldn't that be great," Dennis said, "as long as we didn't have to visit our two friends down the road a ways."

Finally the girls were in the boat and were saying goodbye to their island. "This is a happy day and a sad day," Leslie exclaimed.

"I know what you mean. This has been a great experience. The only sad part is those who didn't survive but other than that, it's been a good time. Well, the fall in the hole wasn't so great," she added.

"No, it wasn't. I was so worried about you, but then you were fine. I hope we get to share a stateroom together. I want to talk with you about some things," she said in a little lower voice hoping that Nathan didn't overhear the conversation. With the roar of the engine, it was unlikely.

When they reached the small ship they unloaded their belongings. Nathan helped so it didn't take long.

"Leave them right there stacked in a pile so it will be easier to transfer them to the big ship when we get there," Nathan ordered.

The navy man hurried back to the island to bring some more of the survivors to the small ship. He certainly wasn't wasting any time. He was an efficient navy officer doing his duty in an efficient manner, the two women decided.

The captain of the boat came over and talked to the two ladies. "You two don't look any worse for the wear. I think you look perfectly healthy for two people who have been stuck on an island for about three months. What ever did you find to eat?"

"There are lots of things on that island to eat," Leslie declared. "For one thing there were lots of berries, roots, bird eggs, deer, bear, salmon and more rabbits than I have every seen in my life. Some of the roots were made into flour so we had pancakes and honey. We didn't starve believe me. And Bethany is a great cook. We found lots of herbs to spice things up. We really ate very well while we were stranded and the nice thing about it is that it didn't cost us a penny." Leslie laughed. She knew they would get a lot of sympathy and they didn't need it. They had a good time on the island.

The captain visited with the two girls until Nathan brought Jim and Dennis over in the next trip. "Do you believe this? I had to ride with the mortician of all things," Dennis remarked.

Jim only nodded his head. He sure was glad that Dennis didn't know before what he did for a living. He would never have made friends with him.

Finally the last boat trip was made and brought Eric, Albert, and Peter. They were a little crowded but they managed. Nathan was tired of going back and forth. Enough was enough. After loading all the suitcases in the small ship, the captain started the ship and headed for the big ship out in the ocean.

All of the survivors stood on the deck and watched their island disappear. Although they were excited about getting home, they almost felt as though they were leaving home. It had been a good stay. They had made friends that would last a life time. The group just kept watching until they could see the island no more.

It took a little over an hour to reach the big ship that would take them back to the United States and home. They all stayed out on the deck and watched the waves, the birds, the view and anything else that they might run into. It was a nice ship ride out to where the big ship was waiting for them.

It took a little time for everyone to get settled once they were at the ship. Bethany and Leslie were going to room together. Dennis, Jim, and Eric had a room together and Peter and Albert shared quarters.

"Boy, I just can't get away from this mortician. Is he trying to tell me something or what?" Dennis asked.

"Since you survived that plane crash, you can survive a few days in a ship with Jim. I find his occupation rather interesting. I'd like to visit your mortuary some time," Eric exclaimed.

"Anytime," Jim answered.

"Forget about me, I'm not visiting. If you want to visit, we can visit at Peter's restaurant that's if he really goes into that business. If he makes enough money on his book he probably will. He talked about how stressful a reporter's life is. I'd have thought it would have been fascinating to meet so many people," Dennis remarked firmly. To him managing a restaurant would be stressful.

"That's probably because you haven't been around aggressive reporters. So far the one on this ship hasn't come around. I wonder what he's waiting for. He'll probably catch us at lunch or dinner time," Albert commented.

Sure enough, just as they sat down to lunch, a man who looked very much like a reporter headed for their table.

"Now that we're all served," Eric said, "Let's pray over the food."

Everyone bowed their head while Eric prayed an extra long pray of thanks for the rescue and thanks for the food and anything else he could think of. When he was through with the prayer, everyone started talking with each other ignoring the reporter all together.

The reporter cleared his throat a couple of times but they kept right on talking. The captain of the ship was headed for the table. When he reached there he asked if he might sit and talk with them.

"By all means, we'd love to have you," Eric stated and the others agreed.

The captain pulled up a chair and waved his hand at the reporter to shoo him away. The reporter left immediately. "I'm going to do my best to keep that man away from you. He wants to hear your story, but when he gets through, it'll be so twisted that you won't even recognize it. I understand there is a reporter among you?" Captain Ryan glanced around.

"I'm the reporter, Captain," Peter admitted. "I actually have our story all written out and I have pictures to go along with it. I just need a computer so I can type the story and send it to my newspaper editor. I sure would like to get mine turned in before this other reporter does his. Mine will be factual all the way."

"My friend, after lunch I'll take you to a room and you can use that computer. If you finish typing before we arrive home, you can send it to your editor from the ship. How would that be?" Captain Ryan asked.

"That's terrific! I'm a fast typist and I think I can finish it before we reach our destination." Peter was excited. He sure didn't want that other reporter to make up a bunch of stuff and get his story published before the true story was printed. He was positive the reporter had a computer with him.

"Now since you're all finished with your lunch, let's take a tour of the ship. That will keep that reporter away for a while longer. Come right this way. The first place he stopped at was the room with the computer. "Now, Peter, do you want the tour or do you want to type?"

"I want to type," Peter answered with a smile. He sat down and took out his notes and began typing. They all stared at him. They could hardly see his hands move. They wondered how fast he was typing. It had to be about one hundred words a minute or so it seemed.

So they left Peter and finished the tour. The captain invited them to his cabin. He wanted to ask a few questions about their time on the island. "The first thing that I need to know is your names. We were supposed to get them with the two-way radios but that didn't work out. I understand that Eric was elected as the leader. Give me the names of the survivors and I'll send them on home so your friends and family can meet you when you arrive in Pittsburg."

"I'm Eric Johnson and this is Bethany McMillan." Eric waited and gave the captain time to write down the names. "This is Albert Desmond..."

"Oh, he was one of them that repaired the engine on the airplane so you could drive it up on the beach. That was great, Albert. You have to be pretty talented to accomplish that. I can imagine how much better that was than the shelter you made from tree logs. Now go on with the names."

"This is Jim Majors, Leslie Morris, Dennis Williams, and Peter's last name is Jameson," Eric stated talking very slowly.

"Now if you'll help yourself to the coffee and rolls while I call this in, then we'll continue our conversation." In only minutes, Captain Ryan had informed the officials of the names of the survivors. He knew that there'd be a lot of people happy and a lot of people very sad that their relatives weren't among the survivors.

"Coffee," Jim exclaimed. "We're going to have coffee. I can't believe it. That was the one thing I missed on the island—my morning cup of coffee."

"Yes, I missed it too," Albert agreed.

Although Bethany usually didn't drink coffee, she decided to join the rest and have a cup. It always smelled so good so she accepted a cup and put some cream and sugar in it. The coffee really tasted pretty good she decided.

"I heard someone say that you built a shelter right away on the first night, is that right?" asked the captain.

"Yes, it was something to do and a place to sleep incase we weren't rescued right away," Eric answered.

"But Nathan said the shelter wasn't there. It looked as though it was torn down. Why did you do that?"

"We didn't but a hurricane did. We had been working on the airplane for a winter haven just in case we had to spend the winter. We weren't quite finished with it when the hurricane came and tore up everything. Our pots and pans were scattered all over along with a lot of other things. But inside the airplane it was calm and peaceful," Eric explained. "The wind couldn't even shake the airplane. Probably the trees were protecting it some."

"You people are the most inventive people I've ever met. You're quite a group and it appears you all get along real well. I saw you praying over the food and I figured that had a lot to do with your survival and your friendship." The captain smiled at the group of survivors. "I sure want to read that newspaper story and Peter's book when it comes out. It will be very interesting."

"We're eager to see the story in the newspaper and eager to read his book too. He did show us the pictures he'd taken. You should see them. They almost tell the story by themselves. We didn't even realize that he was taking picture until the last week or so. He just snapped anything that he thought was interesting. He told us that he had kept a diary of everything that happened to us so it would be easy to make a book out of it. He must be one great reporter," Dennis remarked.

"I'm very anxious to see the pictures if Peter will show them to me. My wife and I have followed your story in the newspaper for some time. Everyone didn't expect any survivors to come from flight 509. They figured the plane landed in the ocean and that was it. Not until you turned the engine of the airplane and fooled with that radio sending the 509 message did anyone have any hopes of survivors. They searched everywhere for you but found no sign at all. The small plane that struck your airplane was able to report the accident before they went down. We thought we might find them floating in the ocean but unfortunately we didn't."

"We didn't know that the tower knew our plane was hit by a smaller one. That was good that the small plane pilots gave that information to the tower," Eric commented. "I wonder if they floated in the ocean with life vests or if they even had a chance to put them on or exit the airplane. The seven of us came out a lot better than the occupants of that small craft."

"I'll say you did. I find the fact that you put a stove in the airplane and had the chimney coming out of the roof rather amusing. When the first airplane pilot said something about that we just couldn't believe it. I want to see Peter's picture of that. It must have looked a little ridiculous," the captain remarked and smiled at the thought.

"Yeah, whenever we looked at it, we had to smile. But inside the plane it looked just like it belonged there," Eric stated.

"That's what Nathan said. That's going to be some news story."

CHAPTER 28

Sailing the Ocean

The survivors slept well that night—that's all except Peter. He stayed up till one o'clock typing his news story. He was ready to send it in the first thing in the morning. Then he decided that he'd start typing on his book here and there. But he did want to join the others from time to time. He just had to get his news story to the press right away before that other joker wrote a twisted version.

When morning came, the group joined the captain at his table. "I want you to join me every meal. That's one way that reporter can't get to you. I'm sure today he'll be looking for any one of you to be walking around the boat and I can't do anything about that but if he gets to be too big a nuisance, I can assigned him to his quarters and not let him out. But I do have to have a good reason to do that."

Captain Ryan kept them entertained and they answered more questions about how they survived on the island. Dining time was especially interesting since they were at the captain's table every meal. They were just thankful that the captain could see their side of things and not side up with that pesky reporter.

After breakfast, Bethany and Leslie headed back to their state room. On the way the reporter stepped in front to them. "Now I need to talk with you ladies," he demanded and stayed put so they couldn't move.

Bethany took Leslie arm and turned her around and they headed back to find one of the men. There was Albert not too far away.

"Albert," Bethany called. "This reporter won't let us go to our state room. Can you help us out?"

Albert walked over to the reporter. Being a tall and well built man rather intimidated the reporter. He was short and thin. Albert stood over him, looked down at him and asked, "Are you trying to stop them from entering their stateroom. That's a bad idea. Ladies, just go on," Albert told them. "Now if you want to talk with someone, you'll have to talk with me. I've been appointed spokesman for the group. You'll receive no information out of any of the other survivors."

The two ladies took off in a hurry. The reporter looked at Albert. He sure would rather talk with the ladies but he would try to get something out of this man. "I want to interview you about your stay on the island. I see that there were two women and five men. That must have made things on the island very interesting. You were fortunate to have two women that survived," the report remarked with a smirk on his face.

"I don't like the way you said that. Those two are ladies in every sense of the word and if you print anything different than that, I'll personally sue you for every penny you have. You'll not find finer young women than those two. For your information, they roomed together at night in their own part of the airplane. We men had our place. Was there something else you wanted to know?" Albert asked in a very strong voice.

"You trying to tell me that there was no…" The report stopped not knowing just how to put it.

"You say that again and I'll take a swing at you. I want you to understand just how special those two ladies are. Now what other subject did you want to talk about?"

"What did you eat?" the reporter asked.

"There were berries, apples, salmon, deer, bear, rabbits and roots that could be made into flour and dandelions that could be made into salad. We ate very healthy food and very tasty with our two cooks." Albert didn't like giving him this much information, but it was better than the reporter making up something and he was sure that was what he intended to do.

Albert stopped and just looked at the reporter. He was a nervous man around Albert as his height intimidated the small man. "They said you had a stove in the airplane. Now I know better than that. You couldn't put one in there if you had one and where could you possibly find one."

"We did have a wood stove in the airplane and we put it in there just like you would put one in a house. We had the chimney and everything. Evidently, there were some people on the island at one time and they left the stove there," Albert stated.

"Now that's interesting. I hear that there was a reporter with you and he's writing the story. I'd sure like to get my story to the news people before he does," the reporter informed him.

"Well, I'm afraid that you're too late. Peter sent his newspaper article in very early this morning with lots of pictures with it. Peter has an excellent newspaper article. He read some of it to us this morning. It's going to make the papers all over the United States, front page and all," Albert bragged.

The reporter's face turned red with anger. He had no idea that Peter could have a computer to send in his news article. Now he had better send what he could right away although he had nothing to send except what little Albert had told him. Perhaps he could catch one of the other men and get some more information. His editor was waiting for the story. The trouble is he'd have received Peter Jameson's news article by now and probably have it printed before he could even send his article in. He sure hadn't counted on a reporter being in the group of survivors.

Reporter John Stimson knew that the captain was doing everything he could to keep him away from the survivors. The captain didn't like him and had even insinuated that his news articles were half false. He had learned a long time ago that you had to spice your stories up a little if you wanted people to read them and he could really spice up a news article.

Jim was sitting on the deck enjoying the view. Leslie and Bethany were with him. John walked over to Jim and started asking him some questions.

"Sir, we all agreed that Albert would be our spokesman. You have to ask him the questions. The rest of us won't answer you so you might as well go back and talk to Mr. Desmond.

John glared at him and he walked away. It was a conspiracy. They wanted the survivor reporter to get all the credit for the news story and they weren't about to help him. Maybe he would write on a different angle. He would watch each one and turn in his own story on what he saw each survivor doing on the ship. That could prove interesting. Perhaps he would see one of the men go visit in the women's stateroom. Now that would be a story different than the other reporter was going to tell.

He kept his distance when he followed someone but they did nothing worth reporting. He might as well have stayed at home. He sure wasn't going to get anything out of these survivors and he couldn't find any dirt to print about them either. That was disturbing. He wanted something to make out that these seven people weren't all that great as it would appear to the public that they were. There had to be another side to the story. But after what Albert Desmond had told him about suing him, he was a little afraid to make up anything just to have a story for his editor.

Eric walked over to where Bethany, Leslie and Jim were sitting and joined them. "Have you noticed the reporter? He has been following each of us trying to see if we do something unethical. I wouldn't doubt but what he makes up something since he can't seem to find anything against us."

"Yes," Bethany agreed. "He follows us but he doesn't know that we know that's what he's doing. I'm sure glad that Peter sent his story on to the newspaper already. It will be in the news papers all over the country by the time we get there. They better send us a copy."

"It was sure nice of the captain to give him a computer to use. Peter said he also was a good ways on getting his book written. I told him he needed to get out here and get some fresh air and he said he would," Leslie exclaimed.

Albert walked up about that time. "Join us," Leslie said. "We heard you had a talk with the reporter and didn't like him too much."

"I almost took a swing at him at what he was insinuating. I also told him that I'd sue him if he printed anything derogatory about our stay on the island. I gave him just enough information to compile a simple story but he sure was looking for some dirt to include in his news article."

"I'm glad we made you the spokesman, Albert. You're bigger and more intimidating than the rest of us. Hopefully, he'll leave us alone now. Say, so far this has been a pretty nice sail, huh?" Eric commented.

"Yes, it's been a lot of fun," Bethany exclaimed. "Where's Dennis?"

"Oh, he was on his way, but the reporter stopped him. He forced him into the lunch room and made him sit down. I wanted to rescue him but I thought I'd just let him talk his way out. Someone should go by and see how he's doing." Eric told them.

"I'm going to sneak in there and see what's happening," Jim said. "I'll be right back. Stay here."

Jim came back laughing. "The captain is in there talking to the reporter and Dennis. The reporter looks very disgusted and Dennis looks very pleased. We sure have the right captain for this trip. I noticed that he keeps an eye on us now and then. I overheard the captain saying something like, if the story isn't truthful, and that's all I could hear. Albert threatened him, now the captain has. We just might be okay with what he writes after all."

CHAPTER 29

The Return Home

While the survivors went their own way now and then, most of the time they stayed together while they were on the ship. They often stayed on the deck and just watch the waves and whatever they could find to see. They really enjoyed sitting in that environment and visiting with one another. The landscape was interesting and changed drastically as they sailed along.

As they visited they knew that they were dreading when they would have to part. That's the part that Eric couldn't understand about Bethany. She didn't at all seem anxious to get home to her fiancé. She seemed more interested in the whole group of survivors than in going home. Leslie and Jim were together a little more than they were on the island and everyone pretty well figured that they were a couple but no one came right out and asked.

The last day on the ship, the group kept together and watched as they sailed right up to the dock. Their families would be waiting as they were told when the survivors would be arriving. Eric suggested that they all go down together so they could say their goodbyes and make a date to meet.

"How about two weeks from today? That's on a Saturday and everyone ought to be able to make it." Bethany suggested. "Why don't you meet at my aunt's house? She has a real big house and we'll plan a fancy dinner. I'll help cook it," she promised.

"Then I'll be there," Albert stated.

"We'll all be there if Bethany is going to cook," Eric promised and the others agreed.

As soon as they stepped off the boat and entered the crowd they each saw their relatives. Bethany's aunt hugged her and cried because she was so happy that her niece was still alive. She had worried lest she was one of those who didn't make it through the crash. She had a big smile even with the tears. It was very evident that she loved her niece.

Eric looked around for her fiancé but didn't see one. He must have had to work or something. If he had been waiting for Bethany to come back, he'd have made it to the ship if he lost his job. He wondered if Bethany was getting a good man for a husband. He'd love to talk to her and try to talk her out of her decision, but it was none of his business and probably she would just listen politely and say nothing.

After glancing around, Eric found his mother and father waiting for him as well as Lisa Brown. He had dated Lisa for sometime and almost proposed before he left on the trip to Europe. Then he fell in love with Bethany and forgot all about Lisa. Lisa was beautiful and his heart gave a funny flutter as he came close to her. He grabbed the young lady and hugged her and then automatically kissed her. Once again she felt good in his arms. How could he have forgotten all about her? There was too much going on while they were on the island he assumed. And he knew he was thinking more of Bethany while he was on the island than he was of Lisa.

Finally he hugged his parents. They both shed tears of joy that he survived the crash and had so many questions to ask. "Let's wait till we get home and we'll talk," Eric promised.

Dennis found his parents and several of his friends waiting for him. He decided that there were some pretty good looking girls in the group waiting for him. It was about time he got married. He had gone pretty steady with a girl at church—Bernice Atwood. He would think about getting married a little more serious than he ever did before.

The time on the island had changed some of his ideas. He figured everyone on that island would be different than they were before the crash. It definitely had made an impression on all of them and that was one for the good. They would appreciate what they had a lot more than they ever did.

Peter had said goodbye to all of them. He didn't have a girl on his mind, only the book that he was writing. He promised to see them in two weeks. By then he would have the book sent to the publisher. He hugged everyone and hurried to his office. He had received a very nice compliment from his editor via the telegram concerning his news article. He was pretty pleased with himself.

Jim and Leslie were holding hands as they left the ship. They were making wedding plans and promised to invite all of the survivors to their wedding. No one was too surprised to hear that. On the ship, they were pretty friendly with each other. Well, the survivors would have two weddings to go to.

Albert's parents were there. He went over and gave them a hug and told them how he had accepted Christ as his Savior. They both had a big smile on their face. Eric noticed that Albert and his parents weren't leaving right away. They seemed to be sticking around for something. He had his suitcases. Perhaps he was waiting for a girl. Albert had been pretty closed mouth about his personal life. Maybe there was a girl after all. He was a good looking man.

Well, Eric knew his parents were waiting so he had to go. Two weeks seem a long time to wait to see his friends again. They all promised to be there so that would be a special time. And it was especially nice to have it at Bethany's place of residence as he was pretty sure she'd do the cooking. He'd miss her cooking and he'd miss her a little too much.

While they were on the ship, everyone exchanged phone numbers and addresses. They wanted to keep in touch and two weeks was a long time to wait to talk with each other.

Eric was home for two days when he gave Peter a call. "How's that book coming along?" he asked.

"Oh, it's going to be one best seller. I'm over half finished more like three fourths through it. I know I can finish it before we go to Bethany's place for a fancy dinner. I'm really looking forward to that time. It will be great to see our island friends," Peter remarked slowly. "I've been busy and that has helped, but I still miss all of you."

"Me, too. Have you heard from anyone else?" Eric asked.

"Yes, I heard from Albert. He told me his parents were so pleased that he became a Christian. He too was looking forward to Bethany's dinner. He sure didn't seem to be upset over her fiancé. I asked if he had met him and he said yes. I suppose now that he's a Christian, he looks at things a little different. He sure is a different man than he was that first day of the crash."

"You can say that again, Peter. Well, I won't keep you. Get back to work on your book," Eric suggested. "We're all looking forward to reading it and seeing just what pictures you included in it."

Then Eric called Dennis. "Say, how's everything with you since you returned home?" he asked.

"Everything is going real good. You should see this beautiful girl I'm dating. Bethany said we could bring friends and I'm bringing Katelyn. We just hit it off. I haven't proposed or anything, but I'm thinking about it when we get to know each other a little better. I knew her before but then I wasn't the least bit interested in marrying anyone. When we were on the island, my thinking changed."

"That's great, Dennis. I've already proposed to Lisa. But we plan to wait a year until she's finished with college. I wonder if Albert has a girlfriend waiting for him. If he has she wasn't at the ship port. At least I didn't see anyone."

"Albert is hard to read. He doesn't seem disappointed in Bethany getting married. He just goes along with it. But he's never mentioned any girl. He just mentioned getting back to his business. Did you know that he owns his own engineering company? Albert is a wealthy man."

"No, I didn't know that. I just know that at first he wanted to be the leader but I think as time went on he realized that this wasn't an engineering project and didn't need that type of supervision," Eric commented.

Finally, Eric hung up. He'd gone to work one day with his dad and today was a day off for the company. That was why he decided it was a good day to check on his friends. He decided not to call the girls.

After he sat down, he thought it would be good to talk with Jim. Good old Jim who was so much help with anything he needed. He was like Bethany in a way, always glad to help in any way he could. He rang the business number Jim had given him as he was quite sure he would be at work.

"Major's Mortuary," come a soft voice over the phone.

He must have a secretary, thought Eric. "Could I speak to Jim Majors if he isn't too busy?"

Jim picked up the phone and said hello. "Eric, I was just thinking about you. Why don't you come down this afternoon and visit me? I'd love the company. This is a slow day and I don't have much to do."

"I'll be right down. To tell the truth, I miss everyone so much I'm having a hard time getting adjusted to this life."

"I know what you mean," Jim said and hung up.

Eric spent most of the after noon with Jim. He wasn't too surprised to find Leslie working at Jim's place. It did him a lot of good to see the two and visit. Perhaps now he would be of more use to his dad at the factory.

His dad hadn't complained but he knew that Eric's thoughts were not on his job. It would take time for him to adjust to his old life after having been on the island for three months with a bunch of very nice people.

His father was fascinated with what Eric had told him about the stay on the island. He had read the newspaper story and had seen the picture of the airplane with a stove pipe out of the roof. He and Eric's mother had a good laugh over that. No, his boy would be all right once he settled down and visited his friends a couple of times. He had never seen Eric as restless as he was since he came home.

Eric felt rather bad that he was so restless. He was glad that his dad was patient with him. He figured once he went to Bethany's house for the dinner and he visited with all his friends, perhaps he would do better. He had never in his life been restless. He just didn't understand himself.

CHAPTER 30

A Surprise Wedding

The two weeks would be up tomorrow. Eric was excited about seeing his friends again. He knew he'd miss them but he didn't think he'd miss them as much as he did. He called the men or they called him several times. It wasn't going to be easy breaking the close bond the survivors has formed with one another.

Eric called all the men and told them that the group should all go over to Bethany's home together. Jim and Leslie agreed. Dennis and Peter said that sounded good to them, but Albert said it wouldn't work out for him but he would meet them here. When the group met at the designated place, they found that even Peter had a girl with him. He introduced her as Melissa Thompson.

Everyone smiled to keep the shocked look from their face. Peter had said nothing about a girl friend and he still didn't comment further. Just introduced Melissa to them and that was it. He didn't even say she was his friend.

They all had decided to dress up for this occasion because they weren't able to do that on the island and this was a very special time. Eric looked at the group. "None of us dressed like this when we were on the island. I'd say we are a pretty good looking group, wouldn't you, Peter?"

"I sure would. I didn't realize I was so handsome until I put this suit on. I don't usually wear a suit. To tell the truth I had to buy one for this special occasion." Peter was all but laughing as he told them.

When they arrived at Bethany's place, they noticed several cars were there. There were people in tuxedos walking around outside. The whole group looked around in surprise. They thought this would only be the group of survivors and their close friends, not a bunch of outsiders. Perhaps it was beyond Bethany's control. Things like that happened. They were sure this wasn't what Bethany wanted.

They walked up to the house and were welcomed in by Bethany. She led them to the back yard that was all decorated for a wedding.

"Bethany, are you getting married today?" Eric asked.

"Yes, I am. That's why there are a few others here besides our group. Please don't be disappointed. I and my fiancé wanted to surprise you. But only the survivor group and their close friends will be at my table at the reception dinner," she promised. "Then we can have a good visit."

They milled around the yard. It was beautiful and very big. Bethany's aunt and uncle must be somewhat well to do, Eric decided. The house was more like a mansion than just a home. He wouldn't mind living in this place. He knew that Bethany only lived here for a short time. She said her aunt invited her after her parents died. But Bethany hadn't added "rich Aunt." He wondered if Bethany had any money of her own. For some reason he didn't think so. She said she had won the trip to Europe in a contest and that was why she was able to fly to Europe. She had also said it was the first time she had been on an airplane.

They looked around and didn't see Albert. They sure hoped he would make it. He promised he would. Perhaps he got stuck in traffic or something. Or maybe he decided to back out because he couldn't watch Bethany be married to someone else. You just never knew about Albert.

The band was set up in the yard and began playing music. They decided to take a seat so they would get one close to the front. They wanted to see everything that was going on during the wedding. It wasn't long after they were comfortably sitting that they heard someone singing a love song. Then the wedding march began. They saw the minister enter. Then they all turned their heads to see the bridesmaids come walking down the aisle.

Then they watched Bethany walk up the aisle with her hand on her uncle's arm. They all gasped a little. She was beautiful before but the wedding gown really made her shine. They didn't think they had ever seen a bride prettier than Bethany.

The survivors watched them as they stepped slowly down the aisle. The colors were beautiful as well as the bridesmaids. Then four men in tuxedos walked close to the archway and stood opposite the three bridesmaids.

"Hey, look at that," whispered Dennis. "It looks like Albert is in the wedding party. No wonder he wasn't able to meet us. Well how about that. I wonder if he's the best man."

"Oh, he's the best man alright," Eric whispered back a little aggravated. "Look where he's standing—right where the groom is supposed to stand." Eric couldn't believe it. Bethany was marrying Albert. If he could, he would walk down the aisle and stop this ceremony. But with the look in Bethany's eyes and the love she appeared to have for Albert, it would do him no good. He wished she had talked it over with him. How did a girl like Bethany fall for a man like Albert? He was good looking all right and he did become a Christian but still he was Albert.

Then he thought back. It was because he saved her life. That was the reason. It wasn't a good reason to marry someone. Poor Bethany, he just hoped that she didn't regret it one day.

"She's making one big mistake," Eric whispered to Jim. "I don't understand this at all. She knows what Albert is like."

Leslie whispered back to him, "Did you ever think that she just might be in love with him?"

"Don't be ridiculous." Then he stopped. The way Bethany looked at Albert didn't look as though she was forced to marry him. She looked like a girl in love. But of all the men on the island, why Albert?

The group watched as the wedding proceeded. When the minister came to the part where he asked Albert if he would take this woman as his wife he remarked, "I sure do." Albert looked so happy and Bethany did too. She was beaming when she walked back down the aisle. Both Albert and Bethany waved to their survivor friends when they passed on their way out. The group smiled and waved back. Leslie was thrilled for Bethany but then she had known that the girl was going to marry Albert and she knew that Bethany was truly in love with him.

At the reception, they saw a smiling Bethany. Her aunt and uncle made over Albert as though he was some one special. The uncle gave a toast. "This is to the bride and groom. We want to welcome Albert into our family. For those who don't know, he's the owner of the Desmond Engineering Company. May God bless this couple and may they find happiness all the days of their life."

The survivors looked at each other. They knew Albert was an engineer but didn't know that he was the owner of that huge building down town. How many times had they passed that building since they came home and never once connected it to Albert.

Finally they all made their way down the line of attendants until they came to the bride and groom. Bethany hugged everyone and then Albert did. He wouldn't settle for a handshake.

"That crash on the island is the best thing that ever happened to me, my friends. I found my Savior there and I found my bride there. Now, Eric," Albert remarked, "I want you to know that we followed your rules and didn't pair off that much but it was hard not to. Once in a while we had a chance to meet where it didn't look suspicious. But thanks to all of you for the great time we had on the island and for how well you treated our two ladies."

Each survivor gave their congratulations to the bride and groom and tried their best not to look too shocked or disappointed. Eric especially had a hard time with the congratulations.

"Where are you two going to live?" Dennis asked.

"Oh, Albert owns a house by the river. After our honeymoon, we'd like all of you to come and visit us. Albert, please give them that card with our address on it," Bethany instructed her new husband.

"Yes, sweetheart, I'll do that." Albert took out his wallet and gave each one of his island friends a card. "We'll be back in two weeks. Can we meet two weeks from today?"

"Yes, we can," Eric said as he looked around at the nodding heads.

When Eric and Lisa walked away from the bride and groom, Lisa questioned him. "Why were you so upset because Bethany was marrying Albert? You acted as though you had a crush on the young lady." Lisa waited to see what Eric would say. She didn't want to be someone he grabbed at because some other girl turned him down.

"Can we talk about this later, away from everyone?" Eric asked.

"That's fine, but I have an idea we need to talk. If you're in love with that girl you shouldn't have proposed to me." She stated this flatly and her voice wasn't all that happy.

"It was just being on that island and taking care of the ladies. You have nothing to worry about, Lisa. I really do love you and want to marry you. I just didn't think Albert was the one for Bethany."

"I'd think Albert was a good catch for anyone. He's handsome and he's extremely rich and famous and he's a Christian. And the way he looked at his bride, you know he loves her. I hope in a year when we plan our wedding, you get her out of your system." Lisa pulled no punches. She had loved Eric for years but he didn't seem to be in too much of a hurry to get married when they were going together.

Eric didn't answer. He didn't want to come right out and lie to her and he didn't want to admit that he thought he was in love with Bethany at one time. Silence was his best answer.

The group once again agreed to meet at Albert and Bethany's in two weeks. This time Bethany promised it would only be the survivors present but they were welcomed to bring a friend. Bethany had taken the time to meet each girl that the men brought to the wedding and gave them a special invitation to come to her house in two weeks. They had an interesting time and a good visit at the reception table.

Leslie looked at the cake. "Have you ever seen any cake as gorgeous as this one or as big? That's some cake. I hope it tastes just as good as it looks."

"I'm sure it does," Bethany said and laughed. It appeared that she had a hard time keeping a smile off her face. She was a happy bride.

When the group left the wedding, Dennis remarked, "Wow that was some ceremony, some reception and quite the fancy place to hold it in. Bethany's aunt and uncle must really love her to give her an expensive wedding like that."

Everyone nodded in agreement and talked about the wedding. Soon they parted from each other as Eric dropped them at their individual homes. Each one was anxious for the two weeks to end so they could visit once more.

Eric was doing a little better at work now. He could keep his mind on his job and do what he was supposed to do. His father had been so glad that he survived that he didn't care if his son worked or not. He just wanted him to get over his restlessness and be the happy Eric he had been since childhood.

When the two weeks were up, each survivor was eager to see the rest. They knew in time, it wouldn't seem so important to meet, but right now they missed each other a little too much.

When they arrived at the Desmond home, they found that Bethany had several of the newspapers that had Peter's article in it. She had placed them on the table. "Did everyone get a copy of the newspaper? If not, here's one for each of you."

Several of them had forgotten about it and were pleased to sit for a few minutes and look over the newspaper and were glad that they would be taking one home with them.

They finally remembered to ask Peter about his book.

"It will be published very shortly. They want it out while the story is still relatively new. So probably in another two weeks you'll find it on the shelf, but don't buy one. I'm giving you each a book. Without all of you there wouldn't be a book. Say, isn't this a luxurious house. I sure didn't know that Albert was this wealthy. You can look right over the river and view a magnificent scene. This is great. I'm glad they invited us over to their place," Peter stated.

"Yeah, when I walked up here, I wasn't sure I was dressed good enough to get inside this a place like this," Dennis admitted.

The survivors had a good reunion. They watched the newly weds. They were extremely happy. Who would have guessed, thought Peter.

Peter suggested that the next time they meet at his house. He would call each of them and he would give them a book. "Just two weeks away and the publishers should send me my requested copies. I get them first before they go to the book stores."

As they left, Eric commented, "I can hardly wait to read that book. It has got to be good. Look at the fantastic newspaper article that he wrote about our crash and the pictures he selected to have with it. I never thought about it then, but that airplane does look a little strange with a stove pipe coming out of the roof."

"I'm going to sit up all night if I have to in order to get it read. I bet he told a lot about our stay on the island. It will be like a visit to the island all over again," Leslie stated.

"When we get the book, it's too bad we couldn't have a slumber party and read it together," Dennis remarked.

"Yeah, I'm sure we want to do that," Jim said. "If you don't mind, by that time Leslie and I will be married and we'll stay up together and have a slumber party by ourselves. Next Saturday is our wedding. Are you all coming?"

"We sure are," echoed the group.

"There's still Eric, Peter and I that could have a slumber party," Dennis suggested.

"How about having it at my place of business," Jim suggested holding back a big smile.

Dennis stared at him wide-eyed and dropped the subject immediately. No way was he going to sleep at a mortuary.

The survivors took the newspapers home and read them way into the night. They were surprised that there were two pages about their survival and all of it was well written. They laughed at the pictures. Peter had picked the best ones and some funny ones for his newspaper article.

They each decided they had to find a way to preserve the newspaper so they could reread it from time to time. That airplane with the stovepipe coming out of the top of it was the best picture yet. When Peter gave them the promised pictures, Eric thought he would frame that one and put it in his office. That would be a conversational piece.

CHAPTER 31

A Nice Surprise

Jim and Leslie had a nice quiet wedding. It was nothing like Bethany and Albert's. Bethany had explained that her aunt and uncle had paid for it and she had to let them do what they wanted to do. She whispered to Leslie that she wanted a simple wedding but her relatives didn't agree. Her aunt and uncle had been so good to her that she didn't want to disappoint them.

The two only took a week for their honeymoon as they wanted to read Peter's book as soon as it came. Peter had called and told them to come to his house in one week and he would have the books.

The week had passed quickly and they all headed for Peter's place. He welcomed them in and as each stepped through the door, he handed them a book. They barely said thanks before they opened it and began to read the first page. On the dedication page they noted that he had personally dedicated it to all of them listing each name. Eric thought that was a nice touch.

They found a place on the couch and each looked through the book and read a little here and there and looked at the pictures. They were all ready to go home and read the book but they needed to visit with Peter first. And then Peter was supposed to feed them lunch. They saw

Bethany coming out of the kitchen carrying a dish of something that smelled so good. Then Albert followed with a big platter of steaks. Peter came in with some more food and finally the table was full.

"Now if you eat and read, you could spill something on the book. Do you think that you could possibly put the book down for a few minutes and eat and visit as well? You'll have all the rest of the day to read the book," Peter suggested. He was pleased that they were so interest in his literary effort but he did want them to eat and visit. The book would keep until later.

Reluctantly, the group did put their books down. But before they did, they had noticed that he had signed the books and written something special in each one of the books. He had written personal notes to each one on how much they meant to him. Peter had done it up right.

Once they started eating, they began to visit and talk about the island and how much they missed their time together. Life would never quite be the same for them. There would always be something missing when they were away from their island friends.

The afternoon passed quickly and before they knew it, it was time to return to their homes. They hadn't made another date to meet as yet but they'd call one another and set something up for a future date.

"We could meet when Dennis gets married, but I hate to wait for ten years," Peter remarked.

"You may just be surprised," Dennis answered. "I think my girl likes me. You just never know."

When he returned home, Eric sat right down and started reading the book. It had over 350 pages and he knew he couldn't finish it in one night. He decided to look and see how Peter ended it. He didn't usually read the end of the book but this was different.

He read: "From the time I first stepped foot on the island and met my fellow survivors, I knew there was something different about Eric and Bethany. They were so peaceful even in the tragic event that had just happened. They appeared to believe they would be taken care of and they had no doubt about that. While I was torn up inside, I didn't say anything. I was just anxious to find a way off the island.

"I was raised an atheist and I firmly believed that we were right in sticking with that belief. But I saw the earnestness of my fellow survivors who prayed over the meals. I saw a beautiful girl go around and do what needed to be done without complaint or fear on her face. I envied that peace she had and I envied Eric that he had such faith in God even though I didn't believe there was a God.

"Then I talked some with Jim and Dennis. They both believed strongly that God had his hand in the crash and that He could have prevented it but He allowed it to happen. That surprised me. Why would a God let something so tragic as that airplane crash happen if He could prevent it?

"Jim stated plainly, 'God doesn't make any mistakes. We may think that it was an error, but God doesn't make mistakes. He didn't cause the plane crash but He did choose the survivors. Peter, just remember, God knows what He is doing.'

"I hung around Albert a lot as I knew he didn't go in for all that stuff and neither did Leslie. But after the bear attack, Albert changed. He was a different man and he had the same peaceful look on his face as the rest of the Christians. And then I noticed that Leslie changed also. They all had a peace that didn't belong to me. When we all sang that song, *I'm so Glad I'm a Part of the Family of God*, I had a desire to be a part of that family. I definitely felt left out. For a Power that I always believed didn't exist, He sure had a great family of believers.

"When we held our last church service on that airplane, I felt something in my heart change. I knew that I could no longer doubt there was a God because I could feel Him talking to me in my heart. I have since asked Him to forgive me and asked Him to be my Savior. Now I have the peace that the rest of the survivors enjoyed.

"I told my parents about what happened and now they are attending church with me. They were so pleased that God had spared my life that they were willing to listen. They now believe. My readers, I hope you believe as well."

When Eric read that, he shed tears. He knew that Peter seemed a little different in that last service but he thought he was sentimental because they were leaving. That ending made the book perfect!

A year later Eric and Lisa married. Dennis and Katelyn had a date set for their wedding. Peter and Melissa had married two months earlier. The survivors attended each wedding.

Bethany and Albert invited all the survivors to come to dinner to their house. They wanted their friends to see little Hillary Alberta

Desmond. Their friends knew that they were expecting and now they could show her off a little.

When they saw the beautiful baby girl, all they could say was that she was as beautiful as her mother. Leslie and Jim paid a lot of attention to the little Hillary. They decided that they wouldn't tell their news just yet. Perhaps in another few months it would be quite evident to every one. But in the meantime they would practice with Albert and Bethany's little one.

Eric looked at the baby and then at Bethany and Albert. They were a good match. He wondered why he was so stubborn before as to not realize that. They had a beautiful home, a beautiful relationship with one another and now they had a beautiful daughter. He had never been so wrong in his life as he was about Bethany and Albert. He loved the lovely lady as a sister now but that was all. God had given him a wonderful wife and he loved her very much.

Bethany was thinking what a great reunion this was. Everyone was single on the island and now they were happily married. She wondered if Eric and Lisa, Peter and Melissa, Dennis and Katelyn, and Leslie and Jim would ever want to go back to the island. She knew the men would but would the wives understand their desires to see the place again? She hoped they could all meet on the island some day in the future and spend a week there. If they did, she hoped they would agree to go by boat. She wasn't quite ready to board another airplane.